THE SPURS OF PALOMINO

Heading to a remote town called San Remo in New Mexico to take up jobs as deputies, Kid Palomino and his sidekick Red Rivers find themselves lost in a deadly desert. Also, unknown to the two lawmen, three outlaws are on their trail, bent on a vengeance which can only be achieved by the death of Kid Palomino. Beyond the desert, a cavalry troop makes a gruesome discovery. Now the wheels of justice are set in motion. Kid Palomino, though, must face his deadliest foe . . .

MICHAEL D. GEORGE

THE SPURS OF PALOMINO

Complete and Unabridged

LINFORD
Leicester

First published in Great Britain in 2001 by
Robert Hale Limited
London

First Linford Edition
published 2003
by arrangement with
Robert Hale Limited
London

British Library CIP Data

George, Michael D.
  The spurs of Palomino.—Large print ed.—
Linford western library
  1. Western stories
  2. Large type books
  I. Title
  823.9'14 [F]

  ISBN 0–7089–4910–X

Published by
F. A. Thorpe (Publishing)
Anstey, Leicestershire

Set by Words & Graphics Ltd.
Anstey, Leicestershire
Printed and bound in Great Britain by
T. J. International Ltd., Padstow, Cornwall

This book is printed on acid-free paper

Dedicated to Irene, John and Paul

Prologue

Juárez had at one time been an important town in Texas in the days when it belonged to Mexico. That had been before the likes of Travis, Crockett and Bowie had slowed up the forces of Santa Anna at The Alamo. Now part of America, Juárez had slid down the slippery slope like so many other border towns starved of everything except hope. Its adobe buildings crumbling with the passing of each season, only the hope of a few stalwart citizens kept faith that Juárez would rise again like a phoenix from the flames of its past and regain its place in the history of the Lone Star state.

This might have come to pass had it not been for the ruthless drifters who had started to use this isolated place as a safe refuge. Gradually, those who remained of the good people of Juárez had to try and cope with the killers and desperadoes who filled their streets. It had seemed as if more and more of the vermin who rode the West, killing and stealing for a living, were gathering within the boundaries of Juárez. The town had tried many things including turning a blind eye and bribery but nothing had worked.

Then two riders had ridden into town seeking a sheriff friend who had long lain beneath the dust on Boot Hill. These men were different from the other drifters who visited the remote, almost forgotten, town. These men had lived by working on the side of the law wherever and whenever their services were required.

These men were called Kid Palomino and Red Rivers.

It had not taken either man long to discover the truth of what was happening in Juárez. Both had stood beside the grave of their friend and wondered who would have killed the old sheriff. Before the pair had walked back into the dusty town, the few remaining members of what had once been the town council approached them.

Red Rivers had not liked anything the people told them about the situation in Juárez but knew his younger friend could not turn his back on anyone in trouble. Kid Palomino listened all through the first night as people described to them what was happening. He did not like any of it.

By the morning he and Red Rivers had decided they could not simply continue riding on to San Remo and the deputy jobs which waited for them.

They had to try and do something to help these people and there was only one way that that could be achieved.

Kid Palomino and Red Rivers had to find the men who had killed the sheriff and left Juárez at the mercy of its deadly gunmen. It had not taken more than a few minutes for Palomino and Rivers to locate the gang. They simply followed their ears and their noses toward the crumbling building which boasted of being a saloon.

The flaking paint on the creaking sign above the porch seemed to warn the pair of the danger within but neither the Kid nor Red paid any heed. They had checked their weaponry carefully before leaving the frightened citizens in the back room of the quiet hotel and were aiming their boots straight at the drinking-hole with a resolve no dishonest man could ever understand or match.

Stepping up under the porch, both men paused and looked briefly at one another for what seemed an eternity. They said nothing as they entered the dark cool interior of the stinking building.

Palomino had expected to see a mere half-dozen gunslingers dotted around the interior, but there were more. A lot more. Standing next to one another the two men who had served the law together for the past five years waited until the swing-doors stopped moving before taking a breath.

Sixteen sets of eyes were trained on them from every corner of the smoky saloon. The sound of females upstairs pretending to enjoy the men who had paid for their services was the only sound to echo around the vaulted ceiling as Kid Palomino and his partner studied the faces.

As they carefully walked across the sawdust-covered floor towards the long bar counter, filled with as many bullet-holes as worm-holes, they knew their presence had been duly noted and was unwelcome.

Reaching the battered bar which was covered in every known deposit guaranteed to attract flies, the Kid paused and stared into the long rectangular mirror which had lost most of its ability to reflect anything.

With Red Rivers facing the seated onlookers and Palomino keeping an eye on the men standing along the bar to his left, they waited.

It was not a long wait.

A man whose face was covered in the

scars which told all who cast their eyes in his direction that he had once suffered the ravages of smallpox stood up from a table and stepped towards them.

'What have we here, boys?' the man asked loudly as he studied the pair.

Kid Palomino turned around until he was looking straight at the man with the scarred features. Palomino recognized the face but paid it little heed as his attention flashed around the assembly of other gunmen.

'Who are you?' the man asked again, kicking a chair before him across the room and raising his hands above the grips of his pistols.

Kid Palomino took one step forward towards the man and lowered his chin as he kept his eyes trained on him.

'The question ain't who *I* am, mister. It's who *you* are.'

Red Rivers stepped beside his partner and glared around the crowd of men who were now also starting to rise from their chairs.

The men who had been propping up the bar slowly edged away and began to fan out around the stale-smelling room as they continued watching the strangers.

'My name's Hoyt Welch and these are some of my friends,' the man with the scarred face announced proudly. 'I reckon even a dude like you must have heard tell of the name?'

Kid Palomino nodded.

'I heard tell of the name. You're the backshooter who killed the sheriff, I'm told. A big mistake, because he was my friend.'

Hoyt Welch seemed about to laugh, but then he changed his mind as the words sank into his whiskey-soaked brain. He spat angrily at the pair of men standing firmly before him.

'I ain't no backshooter.'

'Ain't what I've been told. I'm told you are a second rate outlaw worth a few dollars dead or alive who couldn't beat bar girls in a fair fight,' Red Rivers added, flexing his fingers above the grips of his own guns.

The room went quiet. The men all around the saloon seemed to be waiting for their leader to act. Hoyt Welch took a long time before he finally mustered the courage to go for his guns.

It was his biggest and final mistake in a life which had lasted far too long.

The Kid dropped down on to one knee, drew both his Colts and fired. Then, without a second thought, he fired his lethal weapons at every man who was shooting in their direction. Red Rivers rolled across the sawdust-covered floor, frantically firing his guns too at the men who seemed intent on blasting him and his partner apart.

Within seconds of Hoyt Welch's hitting the floor, half the other outlaws had joined him. Blood sprayed out from wounds as men were thrown backwards by the bullets coming from Palomino's and Rivers's deadly accurate guns.

Acrid gunsmoke darkened the room, and Kid Palomino felt the heat of lead as it tore up the wooden flooring around him, sending smouldering sawdust into his eyes. Knowing he had to make every bullet count, the Kid leapt like a puma beneath a table until he saw the legs of his enemies above him.

Faster than the beat of a heart, the Kid somehow lay on his back and fired both guns up at the ruthless outlaws who tried to shoot him and his partner. One by one they fell all around him until the room suddenly went silent.

Red and Palomino scrambled to their feet and stood gazing at the scene through the swirling smoke. They had managed to defeat the sixteen gunmen without even a scratch to themselves, yet neither man took any pleasure from their handiwork. Slowly walking towards one another through the twisted, bleeding bodies of Hoyt Welch's cohorts, the two men wondered how many bullets still remained in the chambers of their four guns.

Before either of them could utter a word, their attention was drawn to the landing above them, where three more of Welch's gang stood, half-dressed, clutching their pistols in shaking hands.

'Kid! Look out!' Red screamed as he spotted the three men above them aiming their weapons down in their direction.

Seeing the rest of their once massive gang strewn around the saloon in pools of blood made the half-naked trio cock their gun hammers and start firing furiously at Kid Palomino and Red Rivers.

As the lethal lead rained down on them, both the Kid and Red swung their Colts heavenward and started returning the fire. It was only a few seconds later when both lawmen realized their guns had used up the last of their bullets.

One of the outlaws tumbled limply down the rickety stairs, the other two fell over the wooden balustrade and crashed into the sawdust at their feet.

'Is it over, Kid?' Red asked.

Kid Palomino emptied the spent shells

from his guns on to the blood-soaked floor, then reloaded them.

'Get the horses, Red. It's time for us to head on for San Remo. It's over.'

As the pair walked out of the saloon, neither man knew that the words of Kid Palomino would soon come to haunt them.

It was far from over.

1

The magnificent palomino stallion charged up the sand covered hill, its rider holding the reins in one hand and the saddle horn in the other. The tall horse halted on the very summit of the dusty white peak while the rider waited for his companion to catch up with him. Staring out into the blistering sun-baked landscape, the handsome rider, clad in blue denim and a white Stetson, was becoming worried.

What had started out as a mere ride from a train depot to a new town and a new job had turned into something else. Now as the sand began to taunt the young rider he knew he and his partner were in terrible trouble.

The second rider was a smaller, older man with thinning red hair and a matching beard. His brown mount was nowhere as noble-looking as the bigger cream-coloured stallion, but it was just as sturdy. As it too reached the top of the long dune its master reined in alongside his partner. Apart from the beautiful blue sky above them with its cruel burning sun, the two riders faced nothing but one sand-dune after another. It was like being in the middle of a calm, dangerous ocean with no hint of where refuge might be found.

The soft gentle breeze skimmed across the loose white sand of the rolling dunes before them for as far as the eye could see in a haunting, eerie silence. Both riders knew they had made a big mistake in venturing so far into this land. They secretly prayed that it would not be their final error.

For nearly three days they had found themselves heading deeper and deeper into this land of white baking sand. At first they had imagined this was just an annoying interlude on their journey to take up their new jobs as deputy sheriffs in the New Mexico territory. Now the truth of their plight was staring them both in the face. They were well and truly lost.

Now they were beginning to wonder what they had ridden so willingly into after disembarking from the train back at Adobe Wells with their animals and a mere week's provisions.

This was a place where nothing seemed to make any sense to the men who had seen most landscapes in their days of travelling from one job to another. There were absolutely no landmarks of any description. Nothing to work out where they had come from or where they were going. From here, in every direction, there was only hot white sand to burn their tired eyes.

Nothing but sand.

Now they wished there were Joshua trees or simple cactus dotted around as there had been on the first day of their long and fruitless ride. Something to at least give them a perspective on where they actually were. Something to mark their progress or lack of it.

For all they knew, they were riding

around in circles and the gentle breeze which continually blew the top of the loose white granules away was filling the tracks of their horses' hoofs.

There had to be life out there somewhere, they thought, wondering how long their water would last out here in the blistering heat.

They still had some jerky and a few cans of beans left in their saddle-bags but it was the amount of water in their canteens that was starting to worry them. Even though they had brought extra canteens for their horses, they were running low.

Too low.

Kid Palomino sat on his Texan saddle brooding as he watched the shimmering heat-haze mocking them in every direction. When the young man turned his burning body around and looked back down the dune that he and his friend had just ridden up, he saw that their tracks had already disappeared in the whispering sand. Could they have ridden over this long mountain of sand before? He was beginning to doubt even his sense of direction. It all looked exactly the same.

The face of Red Rivers was equally troubled as he sat in his saddle squinting out into the impossible heat haze. Now his tired eyes were starting to play tricks on him as they strained to make sense of what confronted them. Was there really water out there or was it yet another trick of the desert? Yet another teasing mirage?

'There ain't nothing out there, Kid. Or is there?' Red asked, rubbing his face free of the salt which dried in the sun from the continuous sweat which rolled down from beneath his old hat.

'Nothing but sand, Red,' Palomino confirmed.

'We have to find water soon.'

Palomino knew his partner was right. He dismounted slowly from the tall animal and began checking the array of canteens hanging from his saddle horn until he found one which felt full.

'We better water the horses, Red.'

17

Reluctantly the older rider agreed and slid off his tired mount. He began checking his own canteens also. It seemed as if more than half of them were now, like his throat, dry.

'This ain't good, Kid. We have to find water fast or we'll end up dead.'

Kid Palomino removed his white hat, dropped it on to the sand and poured some water into it for the stallion. He took a sip before screwing its stopper back on, then he returned the canteen to the saddle.

'I can't believe there could be so much sand, Red,' the Kid drawled, watching their mounts drinking as his friend moved up to him. 'Nothing but sand. Where the hell are we?'

'Maybe we died and went to hell.' Red tried to grin but his face was too sore from the burning heat which reflected off the white sand.

'You could be right, Red. It sure is hot enough.' Palomino leaned his back against the saddle and ran his fingers through his hair.

'I figure we ought to head there.' Red Rivers pointed his finger straight ahead.

Kid Palomino raised a hand and shielded his eyes.

'Any particular reason?'

'Nope.' Red shrugged as his horse finished drinking from his battered hat.

'Good enough.' Kid Palomino scooped his Stetson up off the sand and placed it back on to his head. The droplets of water felt good as they trickled down his face.

'You figure we'll find water soon, Kid?' There was a tone in Red Rivers's voice which the younger man had not heard for a long time. It was the sound of desperation.

Gathering up his reins Palomino stepped into his stirrup and hauled himself up on to his saddle. He watched his partner doing the same.

'We have to try and look for the signs, Red. There are always signs, ain't there?'

'You mean like birds or something?'

'Yeah, like birds or something.'

'There ain't been a bird in that sky since we started out, Kid.' Red rubbed his face on the back of his sleeve. 'Not even a vulture.'

Both riders knew this was the truth. If there was any life out here amid the endless rolling hills of sand, there would be birds close at hand. The vultures would be waiting for something to die. Eagles would be circling on the hot thermals waiting to swoop down and kill their unsuspecting prey. But there was nothing in the big blue sky above the two men's heads except the blinding sun.

In their heart of hearts, both Kid Palomino and Red Rivers knew that birds would also be hovering some-where above a water-hole, if there was such a thing out here in the desert. To see nothing in the sky meant only one thing.

There was no water anywhere near them.

Red Rivers sighed heavily as he pulled the brim of his hat down in a vain attempt to keep the brilliant sun from burning his already sore eyes. He nodded and gently spurred the horse on down the soft sandy dune.

Kid Palomino urged his stallion on and followed the rider ahead of him. They were in trouble.

2

Adobe Wells was no mere freight stop for the Southern Pacific Railroad, but a precious jewel along the hundreds of miles of dry sun-baked train-tracks. It was the one spot guaranteed never to run dry of water in an otherwise unpredictable territory. A place where there was an abundance of the one thing valued above all others, fresh crystal-clear water. Adobe Wells boasted a mere three buildings dotted along the railtracks, all within yards of the water-towers.

In this oasis in an otherwise cruel land, Adobe Wells's handful of citizens thrived and enjoyed a prosperity not found anywhere else within a hundred square miles. Whilst others in distant places staked claims to gold and silver, these people had found something far more valuable to those who wished to try to traverse its unholy expanse.

They had found the very staff of life itself.

It was no coincidence that the railroad companies had laid their tracks alongside this tiny community. For locomotives, like people, required water. Lots of water.

As the west-bound train slowed to a stop beneath the high water-tower only the steam from its huge boilers made any sound within the small settlement. The hissing of the iron horses had become a familiar and lucrative sound to Adobe Wells and its inhabitants.

Each day brought the massive thirsty locomotives and their equally thirsty passengers and crews. Each day brought more wealth. Yet familiarity breeds contempt among those who know that they have a monopoly of any scarce resource. So it was here in the remote Adobe Wells.

There was a lack of interest among the few people who made their livelihood off the railroad on their seeing yet another train. One man did make the effort to approach the train and greet the guard who stepped down to check his engineer's progress at the water-tower. His name was Treat Wilson.

It was his job to ensure that the guard paid cash for the water, because it was his tower. His water. Others around the small train depot had sunk their own wells but it had been Wilson who, single-handedly, had erected the water-tower.

'Hot enough for you, Treat?' the guard asked, handing over the five silver dollars to the smiling man dressed entirely in black.

'Never hot enough for a man who sells water, Jeb,' Treat Wilson replied as he dropped the coins into his vest pocket.

The guard waved a flag at the coach attendant, who then placed a wooden step on the ground and started assisting the passengers from the train. They all headed for the large wooden building which stood opposite the train bearing the name of SALOON & EATERY over its porch.

Wilson watched the two dozen souls making their way into the building which he also owned, in partnership with his brother.

'You have an hour to eat, drink and powder your noses, folks.'

The guard looked at the engineer forcing the huge tube from the water-tower over the train's boiler.

Suddenly the doors of the freight car at the rear of the train were slid open and three men poked their heads out into the daylight.

Treat Wilson touched the arm of the guard and nodded at the three men standing in the freight car.

'Who the hell are they, Jeb?'

Jeb Cooper removed his peaked hat and dried his brow with a handkerchief.

'Don't know for sure. The older man gives all the orders and the others obey him like he was God or the like,' the guard replied.

'They the law?' Wilson was curious. This was only the second time in a year that he had seen men with horses disembarking from a train. The first time had been only a few days earlier.

'Maybe, but I doubt it. I tend to think they are from the other side of the tracks if you get my drift.' Jeb Cooper replaced his hat and watched the three men carefully encourage their mounts to jump down on to the white ground.

'Outlaws?' Treat Wilson suggested.

'Could be, but what the hell would outlaws be doing getting off a train out here in the middle of nowhere?' Cooper pulled out a small snuff-box, and carefully opened its silver lid. He took a pinch in his fingers and sniffed it up his nostrils.

'We had a couple of riders get off here a few days back,' Wilson said.

'Where was they headed?' Cooper was interested.

'They asked for directions to San Remo.'

'Did you warn them about the desert?'

'I might have mentioned it,' Wilson said, shrugging coyly.

'This ain't the best place to head to San Remo from, Treat.' Jeb Cooper stared hard at the older, wiser man. 'Didn't you tell them that they would have been smarter to stay on the train and get off at Apache Hills?'

Wilson looked sheepish.

'It weren't none of my business, Jeb.'

'You let them ride out from here into the desert?' Cooper sounded disgusted with the wily man. 'I guess you sold them four canteens of water and said nothing at all about the desert. Am I right?'

Wilson grinned. 'I sold them six canteens apiece. Business is business.'

Jeb Cooper could not contain his anger as he marched back along the length of the locomotive towards the three riders who were checking over their horses in the blazing sun. Wilson followed at a less speedy pace.

The three men watched the guard as he approached them with little interest. They seemed to have other things on their minds as they led the horses towards the overflowing water-troughs outside the saloon.

'Hang on there a moment, men,' Jeb Cooper called out. He ran the last few yards until he caught up with the trio.

The older man squared up to Cooper and looked long and hard at the guard.

'What do you want?'

'You figuring on heading to San Remo?' Cooper enquired.

'What if we are?'

'I just thought you ought to know that there is the deadliest of deserts between that town and this train depot,' Jeb Cooper informed the trio. 'Some folks around here might not think fit to tell you that, some folks only think of how much water they can sell.'

The oldest rider released his reins and said nothing as his horse stepped up to the trough and began drinking alongside the others. He was thinking long and hard about the information he had just been given.

Then one of the younger mean stepped forward.

'A desert?'

'Meaner than hell itself, son,' Cooper assured him.

'I don't like the sound of that, Jim,' the younger man said to the older as the third man walked between the horses to join his companions.

Jim Welch was not a man to run away from anything but he saw the warning in Cooper's face as he described the desert and was troubled.

'We are trying to catch up with two riders, mister,' Welch told him. 'Me and my boys here have to catch up with them men real fast. You any idea which way they went?'

'I'm told they headed on into the desert,' Cooper replied as Wilson reached his side at last.

'Then I figure we ought to follow them,' Welch grunted.

'But the two men you seek did not

know how dangerous this desert is.' Cooper glanced at Wilson with the look of disgust still etched on his face. 'Someone didn't choose to warn them like I'm warning you.'

Tom Hart and Ben Black turned to Jim Welch.

'I don't wanna tangle with no desert, Jim,' Hart said.

'Me neither,' Black agreed.

Jim Welch stepped closer to the guard.

'How the hell can we get to San Remo if we don't cross this desert then?'

Jeb Cooper pointed at the train.

'Put the horses back on and then let the train take you to the next stop at Apache Hills.'

'How close is San Remo from this Apache Hills train depot, mister?' Tom Hart piped up.

'A day's ride,' Cooper replied.

'I'm for doing that, Jim,' Black said to the older Welch.

'Me too,' Hart said, nodding.

Jim Welch rubbed his unshaven chin as he thought about the situation.

'Will we get to San Remo before the two men we're chasing?'

Cooper looked hard into the cold features.

'Them two varmints will probably never even get across the desert, let alone reach San Remo.'

Welch spat at the ground before turning to his companions.

'Put the horses back on the freight car, boys.'

★　★　★

Both riders know there had to be an end to the mercilessly hot desert which apparently went on into infinity. Yet there seemed to be none. They had ridden and walked throughout the third day of their journey to no avail. Wherever they were, it looked exactly the same as where they had been the day before and the one before that as well. If progress had been made, neither

Kid Palomino or Red Rivers could tell.

As the sun finally set and to their relief, fell beneath the dunes, darkness spread over them fast. There was no dusk out here in the desert, just light and dark. It was as if someone had blown out the flame of a lantern as soon as the sun had disappeared from view.

Kid Palomino had dismounted and removed the saddle from his faithful mount before the sun had set. Red Rivers sat astride his own horse silently. It seemed that the older man had lost faith in their ever finding a way out of this Godforsaken place. He dismounted only when the sky was filled with countless stars.

Darkness did not bring the relief that the pair had thought would come after suffering the burning rays of the day's sun. For the third night in a row, darkness brought only a terrible coldness which seemed to drill into their bones.

Now it was the freezing cold that

tortured the pair. Anywhere else they might have been able to fend off the sudden drop in temperature by making a large camp-fire, but not here. There was nothing to burn in this barren landscape, not even a few twigs or a handful of dried grass.

So the Kid and Red just sat close to one another sharing a can of cold beans as they huddled beneath their bedrolls.

Wherever they were now, it was not on any map that they had set eyes upon before embarking on this journey.

Had they known of this devilish place when they had set out from the train depot at Adobe Wells, they would have headed straight back to Texas.

Only a maniac would have willingly ridden into this desert as they had done. Their ignorance of the terrain would probably cost them their lives, and they knew it.

Red Rivers handed the can back to his partner and sighed heavily.

'How many miles do you figure we've come today, Kid?'

Palomino scooped the remaining beans out of the can into his mouth with his knife before forcing the jagged lid back into it and forcing it beneath the sand beside them.

'I can't tell, Red. It all looks the same.'

The bearded man began shivering.

'It's too cold to sleep, maybe we ought to use the darkness and try and make some headway. What ya think?'

Kid Palomino was tired but knew the words made a lot more sense than trying to sleep during the hours of darkness when the temperature fell almost to zero.

'You have a good idea there, Red. When the sun comes up, we can make camp and sleep.'

Using every ounce of their energy, the men saddled up their horses again and began to lead the trusting creatures deeper into the unknown. Maybe the darkness would not taunt them the same as the daylight did, for now they were unable to see all the rolling sand dunes going on for ever.

Mile after mile the pair walked with their mounts following behind them. The cold did not seem to get into their bones the same way whilst they kept moving, so they kept going. Hour after hour the two men forged ahead in the soft sinking sand, trying to keep their minds from the realities of their situation.

To dwell too long on their plight was to toy with insanity itself, and they both knew it. As long as they were able to keep walking, there was a chance of making it.

Perhaps salvation was out there in the darkness which made the sand dunes appear blue. Maybe in the bracing chill of night, their brains might have a chance of working this out unhindered by the tortuous desert sun.

The night sky was crystal-clear above their heads as they walked on and on. If they found nothing else in this empty land, devoid of all things except sand, they knew they would eventually find the dawn.

That was their prize. That was the one thing the two men kept talking to one another about. They would continue until the sun rose out from the sand again and tried to torture them, as it had done for so many miles. So many days.

'We'll tie the horses together when the sun comes up and stretch the bedroll blankets over them to make us some shade. Then we'll sleep without getting our skin fried off, Red,' Kid Palomino told the older man.

'That sounds good, Kid,' Red Rivers responded.

3

Apache Hills was a town balanced on a knife-edge. A small creek barely gave enough water to supply the residents who chose to live within its boundaries but it was perfectly placed for anyone who chose to use it as a stopping-off point to reach bigger — more substantial — towns. People used Apache Hills to find cheap whiskey and even cheaper female company but few remained a second longer than necessary. With its dry water troughs and even drier climate, Apache Hills was no place to linger.

It had been dark for nearly three hours when Jim Welch and his two partners led their mounts from the freight car of the huge locomotive down the makeshift platform and headed towards the only building among a small group which was still illuminated.

Even from a hundred yards away the smell of stale beer lingered in the air. The saloon was a large two-storey mud-brick structure. At least a dozen horses were still tied to various hitching rails outside the wide open doorway as Welch reached the porch and tossed his reins to Tom Hart.

Jim Welch stared around the buildings with an eye of someone used to such places. He noted every structure carefully as if his life depended on it. There had been many times during his life when such information had meant the difference between life and death. He had noted that there was no sheriff's office amongst the buildings.

There was, however, a telegraph office directly opposite the bright saloon. Welch looked up at the wires hanging loosely from its roof as they swung in the gentle breeze between the poles that stretched off into the darkness. He did not like telegraph wires because they sent messages far faster than even the swiftest of horses could gallop.

How many times had those wires tipped off the law of his coming long before he had arrived? Jim Welch spat at the ground, carefully drew one of his guns and raised his arm until he was staring along the seven-inch barrel. A single shot severed the wires. He blew the smoke off the top of his gun-barrel and said nothing as he holstered his pistol.

While the pair of younger men tied up the three horses, Welch had already moved to the door frame, where he stood bathed in the lantern-light. He was watching the men inside the saloon with interest as his companions came up beside him.

Jim Welch knew when a place spelled trouble and when it did not. This saloon was busy, yet it posed no threat to the experienced eye. None of its patrons had seemingly moved a muscle after hearing the shot. They were either not interested or were just too drunk to care, he thought. Only the man who stood behind the bar seemed worried by the noise of a gun being fired. He stood sweating as he polished a glass.

'Reckon we'll grab us a few drinks before heading out for San Remo,' Welch said gruffly, resting a hand on the top of the swing-door closest to him.

'They got girls in here, Jim?' Ben Black asked as he stared into the bright interior, trying to focus.

'Girls old enough to be your grandmother. I reckon,' Welch answered. He spat at the ground as he pushed through the swing-doors and entered the smoke-filled room with his men close behind him. The trio made straight for the long bar without deviating a foot in either direction. They were thirsty.

Reaching the bar, Welch pulled his long coat-tails over the grips of his guns before resting a boot on the brass foot-rail which ran along the bar. His older, wiser, eyes studied the faces of those who watched the three as a man polishing glasses walked towards them.

'What'll it be?' the barkeep asked nervously, his eyes focused on the guns of the older man. Many men wore sidearms in this remote territory but few looked as if they knew how to use them.

'Rye. A full bottle,' Welch replied, tossing a couple of silver dollars on to the wet surface of the bar counter.

The man reached beneath the counter and produced a bottle of the best whiskey. He placed it in front of Welch before sliding three thimble-glasses across the wet surface to the men.

'This the best?' Jim Welch asked, studying the label on the bottle.

'You bet, mister. This is the very best,' the bartender replied knowing that these were three customers he did want to risk serving anything but the very best liquor to. His face watched the men as Welch poured out a glass for

41

each of them. The older man downed his drink in one shot and smiled.

'Smooth,' Jim Welch said.

The man behind the bar felt his heart suddenly starting to beat again.

4

Dawn came as swiftly as sundown had done the night before for the two exhausted men. Neither could believe that after so many hours of walking they appeared to be in exactly the same place amid the soft, shifting sand-dunes. They knew they must have made progress but it was hard to believe. Red Rivers leaned against the saddle of his horse as Kid Palomino stopped walking and fell on to his knees.

The sun blazed its way across the white sand and overwhelmed them. The light was blinding to the eyes which had tried to cope with darkness for so many long hours. Neither man dared open them for several minutes as the heat began to rise at its usual unbelievable rate.

Suddenly the cold which had dogged their every step during the night was gone. Sweat now replaced the pain that only intense cold could inflict upon the unprepared. Within minutes of the sun's rising, the men's clothing was drenched in sweat for the third day in succession.

Kid Palomino rubbed his face as if trying to allow the bright light to filter slowly through his fingers until he found the courage to turn and look at his friend. Finally he managed to squint at the older man, whose head was buried on the brow of his saddle.

'Are you OK, Red?' There was concern in the voice of Kid Palomino. He knew the merciless desert was taking a far greater toll on Red than on himself.

Slowly Red Rivers pushed himself away from the saddle and braved the light to look down at his kneeling pal.

'I'm finished, Kid. I can't go on for another minute in this damn desert.'

Kid Palomino knew his partner was serious. There was a despair in the voice of the bearded man that the Kid had never heard before in all the years they had ridden together. Somehow the younger man found the strength to get back on to his feet and stagger to the weary man.

'We ain't licked yet, partner. We'll get out of this damn sandpit somehow.'

Rivers shook his head.

'We're never going to get out of here, Palomino. This place suckered us in and it'll not let us go until our bones are bleaching in the sand.'

Kid Palomino grabbed the shoulders of his friend and shook them until their eyes met.

'We ain't finished yet by a long chalk, *amigo*. You and me have been through too much to let a little sand and sun beat us. We're Texans, and Texans don't quit that easy.'

'I'm tuckered out, Kid. I feel that if I close my eyes I'll never open them again.' Red Rivers could barely contain the emotion which was tearing him apart. He knew it was true that he and the younger man had faced many dangers together, but nothing like this.

'Last night I followed the North Star, Red. I heard tell that's how they steer them big ships out in the oceans. I kept aiming at the star so I know we were headed in a straight line. This desert can't go on for ever and there has to be an end to it someplace. We must be damn close to that someplace by now,' Kid Palomino said forcefully.

Red Rivers shrugged. He had fought many foes but none like this desert. This was something different. He could not fight it the way he had fought their enemies in the past. The outlaws they had faced and defeated in the old saloon back in Juárez were living men. He and Palomino had used their skill to survive that battle, but this was different.

This was no case of living men with guns trying to kill them.

This was a desert.

How could you fight the elements themselves?

46

You cannot hit the sun on the jaw or shoot the sand.

Red Rivers rested a hand on his friend's shoulder and tried to steady himself.

'There ain't no way out of here, Palomino.'

'Believe me, Red, we *will* get out of this hell-hole. Have I ever steered you wrong?' The Kid tried to smile but felt his dry lips cracking with the effort.

'You've gotten us into a few scrapes, Kid.' Red found a smile crossing his bearded face. 'Too many for me to add up on two hands. How do you figure we'll manage to get out of here?'

Kid Palomino drew both the horses close to them and began tying their reins together.

'First we water old Nugget and Derby and then you get some sleep whilst I try and figure this out.'

Red was through arguing with his friend. He nodded and found a canteen with some water in it and handed it to the younger man who dropped his hat

47

on the ground. Red pulled off his own Stetson and dropped it between the forelegs of his faithful horse. He watched as his partner carefully poured water into both hats before the animals lowered their heads and began drinking.

'I'm scared, Palomino,' Red admitted.

The Kid nodded.

'I know, Red. That makes us even.'

5

The three men had decided against riding through the hours of darkness after consuming more than two bottles of the Apache Hills saloon's best liquor. They had commandeered a room each over the saloon. Two of the rooms already had permanent lodgers of the female variety but neither Ben Black or Tom Hart had minded the company. In the dimly lit rooms, both men did what young men do best and cared little who heard.

Jim Welch, who remained alone in his room through choice, nursed a bottle as revenge brewed within his dark soul. Lying fully dressed in his trail gear, the outlaw stared out of the small window at the stars and plotted what he would do to the two men who had destroyed his brother Hoyt's gang back in Juárez.

It was not his brother's having been

killed which really annoyed the outlaw but the fact that three months' planning the biggest job of his life had been blown away in a matter of minutes. Jim Welch had lost a brother, but he had also lost the opportunity of mounting the most ambitious robbery of his career. Sipping at the neck of the bottle as if it were a nipple, the veteran road agent brooded throughout the night.

Sleep to him was something other men did. He had managed to stay fully awake for nearly a week by sheer will power and could not understand why others got tired. To him it was a waste of good drinking time.

Welch had ridden into Juárez with his two younger companions a day after Kid Palomino and Red Rivers had left on their journey to San Remo. When confronted by the awesome sight of his dead brother and the bodies of his eighteen hand-picked desperadoes, Jim Welch had gotten mad.

He had been forced to pistol-whip

the truth out of the elderly citizens of the border town. When he had heard the name of Kid Palomino his blood seemed to ignite inside his veins. For more than five years he had heard tales of the young lawman and his red-haired partner but until seeing his dead cohorts, had not believed any of it.

Now Welch knew it had all been true.

The lawman on the magnificent palomino stallion was no myth created by a dime-store novelist, but a real living, breathing human being. And if he was real, it meant he could die.

Revenge was not something which came naturally to the outlaw but he had his pride. Jim Welch knew he had to seek out and kill the man who had killed Hoyt or he would never be able to hold his head high amongst his fellow vermin.

Kid Palomino and Red Rivers had to die.

There was no other way.

If denied the proceeds of the biggest and boldest robbery ever mounted in

Texas, he would pursue his only other passion: killing.

Welch lowered his legs off the bed on to the floor, pulled his boots over his pants-legs and stood up. He had watched the sun rising thirty minutes earlier but waited until he had sucked the last of the whiskey from the neck of his bottle before acknowledging it.

Now he was ready to tackle the twenty-four-hour ride to San Remo, hoping that the two lawmen had managed to survive the desert so he could kill them himself.

Perhaps San Remo had a bank, he mused. A bank full of fresh-minted money waiting for him and his partners to steal. It was a comforting thought.

Walking out on to the landing, the smell of stale liquor-sodden sawdust filled his nostrils from the large room below. The outlaw stared over the wooden balustrade at the array of empty chairs against the tables. Only the bartender remained sitting behind the long bar, now filled with dirty glasses.

Welch moved along the landing to the first door, turned its handle and pushed it open. The sight of Ben Black lying across the belly of a female old enough to be his mother made Welch thankful he had lost the appetites of youth and preferred to find his pleasures in hard drink. The female seemed to snore far louder than Black and every time her mouth opened her yellow tongue seemed to flap in a void now empty of teeth. It was a gruesome sight.

'Get dressed, Ben,' Welch said loud enough for both the room's occupants to open their eyes. Ben Black waved a hand and slid on to the floor next to his clothes.

'Be right with you, Jim,' Black mumbled, and belched.

Moving to the next room, Welch opened the door and entered quietly. Tom Hart lay on the bed in his long johns, wide awake, staring up at the ceiling with a broad smile on his face. As Welch stepped closer to the creaking bed he noticed the wobbling wig of the female bobbing up and down over the youngster's groin as she knelt on the floorboards. The noise which met Jim Welch's ears could only have come from a mouth that no longer contained a full set of teeth.

Whatever she was doing, Welch thought, it must have cost extra.

As Welch cleared his throat to get their attention, the female raised her head and turned it until she was staring straight up at him. As she smiled, Welch noted the fact she had four front teeth missing. It was not a pleasant sight so close to dawn. 'When ya finished, get dressed, Tom.'

The female began to giggle and adjusted her wig until it was almost straight.

'You want a little fun too, mister?'

Tom Hart raised his head off the pillow and grinned.

'She's awful good, Jim. You ought to let her . . . '

'No thanks, Tom. I don't want to catch nothing.' Jim Welch shuddered. He walked out of the room and headed straight down the flight of stairs until he reached the bar and the same nervous barkeep.

'Another bottle,' Welch said, slamming two silver dollars down on to the bar surface.

'You look like you seen a ghost,' the man behind the bar said. He placed a bottle in front of the outlaw and scooped up the coins in his hands.

'Nope. I figure they were witches, not ghosts,' Welch replied, grabbing the bottle. He drew it close to him. 'Ain't there no young whores in this town?'

'They were young once,' the barkeep said sorrowfully.

'At least you could get some with teeth,' Welch said pouring a measure of the amber liquid into the tumbler. 'Teeth can look real nice in the right mouth.'

'Some folks prefer them without teeth,' the barkeep said raising an eyebrow and looking hard at the outlaw. 'If you get my drift?'

Jim Welch tossed the glass away, lifted the bottle up and started to drink from it.

6

Major Joseph Saunders and his platoon of thirty troopers and two scouts were a long way from the garrison at Fort Grant. Fifty miles away to be exact. What had started as a routine outing around the remote New Mexico settlements and homesteads had grown into something far bigger and less predictable.

Twenty miles from the fortress, the troop had witnessed smoke rising from the distant buttes. At first Saunders had thought it might have been a simple camp-fire, indicating the presence of either a trail drive or possibly even a wagon train. As he led his men towards the smoke, it soon became clear that it was something far more ominous.

Many tribes used smoke to communicate with one another in the southwest and usually it meant trouble.

As the small cavalry patrol headed across the almost flat prairie toward the butte, small clues indicated the true gravity of their situation to the experienced officer. Raising his left arm, Major Saunders halted his men.

At first, he sat alone at the head of the tired troopers, studying the ground before them with eyes which had seen more in his fifty years than he cared to remember.

Joseph Saunders had come a long way since earning the ribbons upon his chest during the war. He had seen enough death to last him a lifetime after the end of that conflict, which pitted brother against brother, year after bloody year. Others had quit to go back to their homes up north but not Saunders. He had chosen to travel west to the new lands which were opening up for the ceaseless hordes of settlers looking for a new life to replace the one they had lost.

Men of Saunders' bravery and experience were sent to places like Fort

Grant. What had seemed at first like a peaceful place to see out his commission until retirement rewarded him for all those bloodstained years, had turned into something less tranquil.

After five years of seeing the treaties with the various Indian tribes being ripped up when it suited those back East to do so, Saunders had found himself battling day after day, trying to prevent the inevitable.

Joseph Saunders knew the rancid aroma of war only too well and he could smell it growing stronger as each week went by out in the prairies of the New Mexico territory.

At first it was one tribe pitted against another as they desperately tried to live within ever-shrinking boundaries. Then it was the vengeance of certain Indian leaders as they began to resent the white intruders who continually took everything away from them. First it was their land and then their very way of life itself.

Things were at boiling point and

Saunders knew it.

Yet Saunders was a man who had to do as his masters commanded however much it sickened him. He had to punish those who had the courage to object to their own extinction.

So many tribes had been herded into this arid landscape that it was inevitable that they would start to rebel. The treaty-breakers back East just assumed that if you forced entire tribes into lands which could not sustain them, they would do the decent thing and die. Saunders knew there were more than a few who preferred to fight and die rather than just die.

Saunders gazed down at the ground before them. The signs were there for anyone to read, as long as they understood them. He did.

Innocent drifters might not have seen anything untoward amid the sagebrush and tall cactus which dominated this cruel terrain. Saunders's honed senses told him something different.

'What is it, sir?' Sergeant Bruno

Dean asked as he spurred his horse closer to the major's mount.

Saunders stared out at the distant butte and the smoke which drifted a little on the still air. He knew something had happened but was not sure when or who had done it.

'Does that look like regular smoke to you, Sergeant?'

The big sergeant tilted his head as if he might gain a more accurate view of it that way.

'Could be a couple of drifters frying some bacon, sir.'

Saunders turned his head and stared across at the soldier.

'It don't look like Indian smoke to you?'

Bruno Dean pondered.

'Yeah, it does kinda look like that too.'

Leaning on the cantel of his saddle, Major Saunders turned and looked back at the two Indian scouts who sat upon their ponies next to the bugler. They were full-blooded Crow and had been at Fort Grant longer than Saunders himself.

'Smiling Joe, Rooster, come here,' the major ordered.

The pair of scouts rode their horses up to two soldiers hesitantly. They had been watching the smoke, like Saunders. They too knew something was happening.

'You see that smoke, boys?' Saunders pointed.

Both Indians nodded.

'Can you read it?'

'No can read,' Rooster said drily. His eyes flashed to his fellow Crow.

'Just smoke,' Smiling Joe added.

'You ride and find out what is going on over there.' Saunders saw the fear in both their eyes. He recognized fear because like all heroes, he had experienced it many times himself over the years.

The scouts grunted and rode their ponies off into the brush at a speed he had not seen them use before.

'Do you trust them Crow, sir?'

Sergeant Dean asked, feeling the effects of the morning sun bearing down on his large frame as he sat astride his horse.

'I tend not to trust anyone, Sergeant,' Saunders replied honestly. He turned again to face his men. 'Dismount.'

Bruno Dean lowered himself on to the ground and watched as the major dismounted, then suddenly knelt down a few feet ahead of his horse.

'You seen something, Major?'

'Yep. I've seen plenty.'

'What?' the big soldier asked.

'Signs, Sergeant. Plenty of signs.' Saunders removed one of his white gauntlets and touched the sandy ground.

'What kinda signs?' Dean leaned over his superior officer and tried to make out what was so interesting. 'I don't see nothing at all.'

Joseph Saunders rose slowly to his feet and stared around them before answering.

'Smiling Joe and Rooster ought to

have seen this. Maybe they did but were too scared to mention it. They did seem troubled.'

'What did they see?' Dean rubbed his neck, feeling the frustration welling up inside him.

'Something which they did not want to admit, even to themselves.' Major Saunders rested his hands on his gleaming black belt. 'Something so horrific that two full-blooded Crow Indians tried to pretend it did not exist. Smiling Joe and Rooster wanted us to ride over this ground and get to a safe haven.'

'It must have been pretty bad for them two boys to be scared, sir,' Dean said, and sighed heavily. 'I've known them for years and they ain't the sort to lie to us troopers.'

'They didn't lie. They just tried to avoid the truth,' the officer told him.

'The truth about what, sir?'

'There was a fight here, Bruno. A big bloody fight. Even I could see it in the sand but our scouts did not appear to notice it.' The major ran his fingers over his jawline.

'I don't see nothing, sir.'

'I've seen too many battlefields in my days not to be able to spot the tell-tale signs of one in this climate. Blood tends to be absorbed into sand but it don't go away.' Saunders led the bigger man away from the other troopers. 'This entire area is covered in dried blood.'

'It is?' Dean swung his head around trying to see the clues which the older man seemed so certain about. He still could not see anything at all.

'I figure at least twenty men were slain on this very spot not more than a week ago,' Saunders stated.

'But where are the bodies, Major?'

'We're standing on them, Sergeant. We're standing on them.'

7

Kid Palomino had rested as his friend slept beneath the blankets spread between the two saddles of their horses for nearly three hours. It was crude but gave all the protection of a real tent as the sun slowly crept up into the blue cloudless morning sky.

The shade seemed to take the fire out of the blazing rays of the sun and Red Rivers slept peacefully beside the thoughtful Kid. The younger man knew that all his partner's fears were closer to the truth than anything he had managed to say.

Somehow they had ridden into the very bowels of hell itself and there did not seem any way out for either of them. It was like being a fly trapped in a spider's web. However much they tried, they were unable to free themselves. Maybe the desert ended over the next dune or the one after that, the Kid thought as he watched his snoring pal sleep.

They needed a miracle.

The sand was still whispering its secrets all around them in its taunting fashion but only the younger man listened. He was thankful to see Red sleeping. Whilst asleep the older man could not think about their plight and fret.

It seemed impossible but it actually felt hotter to the Kid than the previous couple of days. The heat-haze made shimmering images dance before his tired eyes a mere twenty feet away on the ridge of the closest dune. It was like looking into a wall of moving water.

Water.

The word was starting to haunt him.

Kid Palomino knew they now had less than a full canteen of the precious stuff between them. Enough for the horses but nowhere near enough for them all to last out the day.

Then something caught his eye

beyond the mirage which moved continuously before him.

At first he thought it was just his fevered imagination playing even more tricks on him. How could he believe anything he saw out here any longer? Palomino dropped his face into the palms of his hands and rubbed at his eyes before raising his head up once more.

Whatever it was, it was still there.

Why didn't it stay still long enough for him to focus upon it? he wondered.

What was it?

Kid Palomino began to doubt that there was anything there at all except the imaginings of a tired mind starved of rest and water. Yet however much Kid Palomino tried to take his eyes off the vision he was compelled to continue looking. Somehow the Kid managed to rise to his feet and step out from beneath the makeshift tent.

He kept looking at the image trying to make sense of it as he brushed the sand from his clothing.

The taunting black shimmer changed shape every few seconds on the very ridge of the dune.

Kid Palomino felt a sudden trepidation gripping at him. He had heard tell of men who had been lured to their deaths by such things. There came a point when men lost their minds in situations such as the one he was in. He knew he was close to reaching that point as he stepped along the side of his stallion and began fumbling with the blanket until he found what he was seeking.

Reaching to the array of canteens, he found one with a little water still in its belly. He unscrewed the stopper. There was less than a mouthful left but he poured it into his mouth and swilled it around his teeth before swallowing slowly.

It felt good. Darn good.

Hanging the empty canteen back on the saddle horn he returned his attention to the dune and could still see the strange image floating in the boiling air.

It was real, he thought. Whatever it was, it was real.

As the water refreshed his tired body, he found himself walking away from his sleeping partner and the two horses. Like a moth being drawn to the light, Kid Palomino slowly ascended the soft sand towards the vision.

The sand seemed to give way beneath the weight of his body several times before he reached the top of the dune but he managed to make it all the same. As he stood looking at the magnificent image which had played tricks with him, he finally began to realize what it was.

At first he only saw the shape, but then his brain managed to work it out.

The painted pony with eagle feathers hanging from its mane should have alerted him, but the Kid was too weary. As he focused on the rider he began to nod. The proud face of the near-naked warrior seemed carved from mahogany

70

as it jutted from the long braided black hair. The rifle decorated in rawhide was just visible from behind the round war-shield.

'Howdy,' Kid Palomino said. He stood before the impressive Comanche warrior trying not to look as feeble as he actually felt. He had seen Comanche warriors before and recognized the intricate designs woven into the beaded shield the man held so proudly.

Menacingly, the Indian raised his leg over the neck of his mount and slid from it on to the sand still clutching his rifle and shield in one hand whilst keeping the other concealed from Palomino's view.

With hooded eyes that never appeared to blink, the Comanche stared at the figure of Kid Palomino for a few moments. There was a nobility about the Indian as he stepped closer and closer to the weary lawman.

It suddenly dawned upon the Kid that this heavily armed brave was bearing down on him and yet he was unafraid. Maybe the desert had drained not only every ounce of moisture from his body but all of the fear too.

The Comanche began to speak.

'You hunt for me?'

'Nope,' Kid Palomino answered honestly.

'Then why you here?'

Palomino shook his head.

'Me and my friend are lost.'

'Other man not dead?' the warrior asked, pointing his rifle down at the sleeping Red.

'Me and Red are damn close to death, my friend.' Kid Palomino felt his throat tighten as thirst gripped at his words.

The Indian reached to the neck of his beautiful horse and pulled a huge leather water-bag down with his free arm. It was moist and swollen.

'Blue Snow has water. You drink.'

Kid Palomino's hands trembled as he accepted the heavy bag.

'Thank you, Blue Snow.'

8

Major Joseph Saunders had been right. Beneath the feet of his cavalry troop were the bodies he had spoken of. After uncovering three of them, he ordered his men to rest and make camp. It was nearly noon and the experienced cavalry officer knew troopers with full bellies were a lot more reliable than hungry, tired ones. The New Mexico sun had a harshness about it which took very few prisoners and Saunders wanted his men and horses fresh before they continued. Due south lay the merciless sand which many men had ventured into, never to return. Major Saunders wanted his men capable of performing their task fully rested and able to survive whatever fate threw at them.

Sergeant Bruno Dean looked hard into the eyes of his superior officer as

73

they walked away from the third of the bodies they had uncovered.

'Who could have killed them Apache, sir?'

'Only two were Apache, Sergeant Dean. The third was a full-blooded Comanche warrior,' Joseph Saunders corrected the burly man.

'Indians are Indians, sir. What difference does it make if they was Apache or anything else, for that matter?' Dean sniffed at the dry air which was painted with the aroma of death and decay.

Saunders swung around and glared straight at the sergeant.

'It matters a great deal if you want to be able to live until this time tomorrow. Out here we have ourselves a lot of different tribes competing for this waste land. Each tribe has its own ways and rituals. Never let me hear you underestimate any of them again. The Apache fight one way but the Comanche another. To survive an encounter with them, we have to know our enemy.'

'I just meant that it don't concern us

none if'n they kill each other.' Sergeant Dean shrugged. 'Kinda saves us a job.'

'It concerns me greatly that you continue to display no respect for them.' Saunders rubbed his face as he watched his men preparing to cook a meal whilst others unsaddled and watered their horses. 'There are many Indians out here who are far from their original homes. Each of them has a darn good reason to be a tad angry with us.'

'But why?'

'Those folks back in Washington make the laws but it's us who get paid to enforce them,' Saunders said, and sighed heavily.

'But what difference does it make whether we are facing one tribe or another, sir?' Sergeant Dean rested his thumbs in his yellow suspenders as his fingernails scratched his belly.

'Comanche use their horses when they fight. They are the best horsemen I've ever come up against. To fight them, you have to know this,' the major answered. 'The Apache fight totally differently. If you try to defend yourself against them, you have to adapt. To confuse one with the other would be fatal.'

'How come you seemed so worried about finding the body of a Comanche out here, Major?' Bruno Dean still could not work out what was concerning the officer so much.

'Because Comanche don't usually come this far west,' Saunders answered. He felt his heart racing as he remembered the first time he had encountered the notorious Comanche nation. It had been a brutal fight which was branded into his memory. His entire regiment had been taught a very telling lesson that fateful day. One that Saunders did not want to repeat.

'For all we know, the Apache just licked a Comanche hunting party, sir.' Sergeant Dean rested his hand on the bridle of his mount and looked into Saunders's eyes. The officer's words had not really been understood by the large brutish man. He still believed that the only way to deal with Indians was to kill them before they killed you. It was a feeling which was common amongst the enlisted men of Fort Grant.

For Major Saunders the sight of that Comanche warrior in the shallow grave had rekindled thoughts he had long tried to forget. Thoughts which tortured him.

'We'll find out if your theory is correct later this afternoon when we dig up the rest of the bodies,' Saunders announced bluntly.

Bruno Dean closed his eyes.

'We're gonna dig them all up?'

'There seems to be one thing you have over-looked, Sergeant,' the major said coldly.

'What, sir?'

'Neither Apache nor Comanche bury their dead this way. It's against their religion,' Saunders said bluntly. 'So whoever did bury these bodies was certainly no Indian.'

The face of the large sergeant went pale.

'Then who did bury them, Major?'

'The question is *why* did they bury them,' Major Saunders said. 'And what are we up against?'

9

Jim Welch rode as he lived, fast and furious. Somehow his two companions managed to keep pace with the older rider as they headed along the well-used trail which connected Apache Hills with the distant San Remo.

The horses continued galloping along the dusty road between the tall chaparral even though their every instinct told them to rest, for needle-sharp spurs forced them on and on.

It was as if Jim Welch wanted to reach San Remo before nightfall even though he and his partners knew it was an almost impossible task.

Finally, as his horse began to stagger from exhaustion beneath him, Welch drew in his reins and stopped the mount. Dust seemed to drift over the snorting horse long after it had ceased thundering down the endless road.

Upon catching up with their leader, Tom Hart and Ben Black halted their own horses and quickly dismounted. They watched the angry face of the outlaw staring at the long winding trail before them. It seemed that Welch hated not only this journey but the very land itself.

'We gotta rest these critters, Jim,' Hart said. He threw his stirrup and fender over his saddle and unbuckled the cinch strap. 'They're spent.'

Black said nothing as he copied the actions of Hart. He watched as Welch reluctantly stepped off his horse and kicked at the ground.

'They said it was a twenty-four-hour ride to San Remo. I got me a gut feeling it's gonna take us twice that time before we manage to get there, boys.'

The three men looked at one another for a few moments. It was as though they knew the words were true. This was no twenty-four-hour ride to San Remo as the train guard had told them back in Adobe Wells. This was a trail which wound through some of the most fearful of terrains as it skimmed the deadly desert of pure white sand. Although all three knew their journey was going to take them far longer than they had originally planned, only the younger two seemed unconcerned. Welch looked and sounded angry.

'It don't matter none. We got plenty of time.' Tom Hart smiled as he dragged the heavy saddle off the back of his sweating horse. Steam rose into the hot air as he dropped the heavy weight on to the ground and tied his reins firmly to it.

'Take it easy, Jim. We have all the time in the world to get to San Remo,' Ben Black said. He pulled his own saddle off the back of his mount and laid it on the dusty road.

Jim Welch did not agree with either of his men. He wanted to be out of this prairie before the sun set. He knew there were many things in this strange landscape that meant danger and even death to the unwary. They had no more than five hours of daylight left, possibly even less. Welch was uneasy.

'They must have fixed those telegraph wires by now back in Apache Hills,' Welch said, looking up at the nearest pole with its swaying wires. There were so many of them dotted along the entire length of the trail.

'You figure that they wired ahead to tell them we was coming, Jim?' Hart asked.

Jim Welch pulled one of his pistols from its holster and aimed it carefully at the top of the closest telegraph pole. Squeezing the trigger, he watched as one wire was severed and fell into the brush which edged the dusty road. Then he fired again and brought the second wire down.

'Now if they wanna talk to San Remo they'll have to come all the way out here to fix it,' Welch said, sliding the gun back into its holster.

'You look a mite worried, Jim,' Tom Hart noted quietly as he studied the nervous man.

'I don't wanna be out here after dark, boys,' Welch admitted reluctantly.

Hart turned and looked hard at the veteran outlaw. He could not disguise his surprise.

'How come, Jim? Are you afraid?'

Welch took three steps toward the younger man and smashed a gloved fist into Hart's jaw. Hart hit the ground hard.

'Nobody says that Jim Welch is scared of anything. You understand that, *amigo*?'

Tom Hart rolled on to his knees and checked his jaw before rising to his feet and backing away from the stronger man with the clenched fists.

'Easy, Jim. I ain't for fighting with you.'

Ben Black said nothing as he removed one of his canteens from the saddle at his feet and began unscrewing its stopper.

'You boys don't have the brains to be weary of this land like I have. This ain't the sort of place you wanna be in after sundown,' Welch snarled. He strode around the two men kicking at the bone-dry ground.

'How come?' Hart asked. He spat out a mouthful of blood and continued checking his bruised jaw. 'This don't look no different from Texas except the cactus are taller.'

'There are critters out here. Poisonous critters,' Welch replied. 'I seen a man bitten by one them critters once. His head was the size of a stew-pot and all black within half an hour. I don't know what bit him but whatever it was, it was deadly.' Tom Hart glanced at Ben Black who was sipping from his canteen silently. Then they began to take more interest in the strange vegetation that surrounded them.

Both men suddenly were very afraid.

10

Somehow the Comanche warrior looked totally unaffected by the desert which surrounded them. Unlike Kid Palomino and Red Rivers there was no trace of sweat upon his gleaming skin. Blue Snow had willingly given the two lawmen his large leather water-bag and sat next to his pony watching as Kid Palomino and Red Rivers had used the water to refresh their horses and themselves.

For more than half an hour the Comanche had said nothing as the sun drifted ever lower in the afternoon sky. He had just watched the pair of white men trying to regain part of what the cruel desert had taken from them since they had entered its deadly womb.

As the Kid felt the effects of the water bringing him back from the brink of death, he wondered about the elegant Indian who said little but watched everything. Where had he come from? Why was he here? Why would he willingly share his precious water with strangers? There were so many questions filling the young mind of the lawman as he checked his magnificent stallion.

Red Rivers had said little since being awoken. At first he had been terrified by the sight of the well-built Comanche but soon realized this man had saved both his and Palomino's lives by showing up when he did.

'You alone, Blue Snow?' Rivers asked as he led Derby towards the seated brave.

Blue Snow nodded slowly.

Kid Palomino teased the reins of Nugget and walked the tall horse up to the others. Now their shadows were long and black as yet another day began to die.

'I ain't never heard of a Comanche brave riding alone, Blue Snow,' Palomino said. He held on to the horn of his saddle and watched the warrior.

The Comanche rose to his feet and walked around the stallion, quietly admiring the beautiful horse. He had seen only a few horses like it before and he envied its owner.

'I not alone at beginning. Now all my brother Comanche are dead.' Blue Snow sighed and he ran a hand along the cream-coloured coat of the horse.

'Were they killed?' Red asked curiously.

Blue Snow nodded again.

Kid Palomino turned and faced the impressive man.

'Who killed them, Blue Snow?'

'No more talk now,' Blue Snow said bluntly. He walked back to his own pony and grabbed a handful of its mane in his hand and swung up on to its back. 'We must go.'

Palomino stepped into his stirrup and mounted Nugget. He could see there was a lot of pain in the hooded eyes of the handsome Indian yet wondered why he would not tell them the rest of his story. Was it just too painful to go into detail? The young lawman was curious.

'Should we be worried?'

Blue Snow said nothing until he had watched Red Rivers hoist himself on to the back of his horse. Then he allowed the pony to walk between the two larger horses and pointed his finger in a north-easterly direction.

'We go that way,' he announced.

The two lawmen tapped their spurs into the sides of their horses and followed the painted pony across the soft dunes. Neither rider was about to say anything to the Comanche who seemed to have many untold secrets.

One of which was how to get out of this blisteringly hot desert.

★　★　★

Major Joseph Saunders stared down at the dial of his golden hunter watch. It was two minutes before four. Snapping the lid shut he slid it back inside his left breast-pocket and secured the silver button just beneath the line of military ribbons.

It had been a gruesome few hours for the troopers.

They had uncovered exactly eighteen bodies buried a few inches beneath the sand. Six Comanche and the rest Apache. All had been killed by deadly accurate shots to the back of the head. Apart from the fatal wounds there appeared to be no other sign of injuries.

Slowly the officer began to realize his first assumption was wrong. There had been no battle. No gallant fight between men of equal might.

There had only been an execution.

Perhaps eighteen individual cold-blooded executions.

But why? The question tore at his very soul.

Saunders walked from one body to the next trying to work out who had done this awful thing. Each step allowed his eyes to focus on the next victim, and then the next. Who could or would do this? The longer he pondered the question, the less convinced he was of his theories. There was an insanity about this carnage which troubled the major. Saunders had witnessed many massacres in his long career, perpetuated by men of all colours and creeds, but this was different.

'I figure we ought to head back to Fort Grant, Major,' Sergeant Dean said, trying to mask the smell of rotting flesh from his nose with his huge hands.

Major Saunders did not reply. He just kept walking from one body to the next trying to find the smallest of clues as to who could have done this to so many experienced fighting men. Neither the Apache nor the Comanche braves who lay before him had been stripped of any of their valuables. Gold and silver necklaces and bracelets still adorned the corpses.

It was a mystery.

Saunders did not like mysteries.

They stopped him sleeping at night. They played on his mind like puzzles.

He was not a man who could turn and ride away from so many unanswered questions.

'We are not returning to the fort just yet.'

'Is that wise, sir?' Sergeant Dean asked as he walked slowly behind the officer.

'I'm not leaving here until I've solved this damn mystery, Sergeant,' Saunders said looking up at the big man and the cavalrymen who stood behind him, still holding their army-issue spades.

'Maybe we ought to go back and get reinforcements?' Bruno Dean suggested.

'I think not,' the major muttered as he carried on walking around the bodies which had started to attract flies.

The face of every trooper seemed to go blank at the thought of their staying out here in a place where deadly killers might be waiting for fresh victims.

'But, Major,' Sergeant Dean raised his voice, 'what if the scum that did this come back?'

91

Saunders stopped moving and rested his gloved knuckles upon his hips. He thought about the question for a few moments before turning to look at his troop. The sun was now very low and long dark shadows trailed across their anxious faces.

'Saddle the horses, men.'

Dean stepped closer to the major.

'Did you change your mind, sir?'

'No. We are not going back to our cosy cots at the fort. We are heading on out there.' Major Saunders raised his hand and pointed toward the hills. 'Whoever did this is out there.'

Dean swung around and marched toward the troopers. He ushered them towards their horses.

'You heard the major. Get them saddles on them horses.'

Joseph Saunders shook his head and followed his men towards the line of waiting mounts. He had seen enough bodies for one day and prayed he would not see any more.

Suddenly there was the sound of two

shots ringing out in the desert. The troopers rushed to their stacked rifles and armed themselves as the noise echoed in their ears. Only Saunders remained calm as he approached the nervous soldiers.

'What was it, sir?' one of the kneeling cavalrymen asked as the officer paused behind him.

'Nothing for you to worry about,' the major said, patting the young man on the shoulder.

Sergeant Bruno Dean stared up in the direction of where the shots had come from and knew that was where the two Crow scouts had ridden.

'Get the horses readied, men. Whoever fired those shots seems to have quit,' Saunders said, staring out towards the butte where the smoke he had sent his two scouts out to investigate, had stopped rising.

Sergeant Dean stepped beside the major as the enlisted men hurried to saddle all their horses. Leaning close to the officer, Dean whispered:

'It strikes me that them shots came from where we sent Smiling Joe and Rooster, sir.'

'I was thinking exactly the same thing,' came the quiet reply.

11

The three riders reined in their lathered-up mounts and stared nervously around the sun-bleached landscape, trying to work out where the sound of two shots had originated a few minutes earlier. To their right a low butte seemed the most obvious choice but none of the ruthless trio had any intention of trying to find out for certain. Apart from the dusty trail, this prairie was covered in towering cacti and all sorts of other lethal-looking vegetation. Each man knew he would have more chance trying to ride through barbed wire than any of that after sundown.

The sun now hung just above the horizon and glowed with a red hue of awesome intensity. All of the riders shielded their eyes from the blinding rays and swung their mounts full circle as they listened to the haunting echoes of gunfire.

The men drew their mounts close together and vainly attempted to work it out. It was an impossible task.

'Well, I figure that we ain't alone out here in the Godforsaken prairie, boys,' Jim Welch said drily as he tried to keep his skittish horse under control.

Tom Hart held on to his Winchester as his eyes darted from shadow to shadow, seeing things which only terror could visualize.

'Two shots. I heard two shots, what about you?'

'I heard maybe three or four,' Ben Black said as he rubbed the dust and sweat off his face with the back of his gloved left hand.

'There were only two shots. The rest were just echoes Ben,' Welch said. He teased his mount ahead and looked at the sun dipping towards the ground along the dry trail. Night was coming and the hardened outlaw felt uneasy. This was no place for men to spend any time in after sunset.

'Who do you figure is out there, Jim?' Tom Hart asked anxiously.

'Maybe the law. Maybe just someone hunting his supper,' Welch answered. His words were firm but lacked conviction. He knew it was unlikely that there would be hunters out in this land so devoid of water-holes. Even animals had the brains to stay out of this sort of place. And if there were no animals worth eating or skinning, there would be no hunters.

Tom Hart's face seemed frozen in terror. He jabbed his spurs into his horse and moved closer still to the older man.

'I heard tell that this country is stinking with Indians, Jim.'

Welch turned his head and looked at the face of Hart.

'Yeah, it could have been Apache, I guess. I heard that there are a lot of Apache in New Mexico.'

'Apache?' Black felt the hairs on his neck tingle as he repeated the word.

Robbing banks and killing innocent people was one thing but facing Apache was another. 'I don't wanna tangle with no Apache, Jim.'

'Neither do I, Ben. Trouble is we ain't dealing the cards in this game,' Welch said thoughtfully. He continued to stare at the butte where he was convinced the shots must have come from.

'What the hell have we ridden into here, Jim?' Hart whined.

'We ought to head back to Apache Hills and catch the train for Texas,' Ben Black urged the older man. 'We ain't Indian fighters and you know it.'

'Kid Palomino is probably already in San Remo sitting in a saloon sucking suds and drinking beer, boys,' Welch snarled. 'Him and me have a score to settle. I ain't turning back until he's paid for what he did to Hoyt and the rest of the boys back in Juárez. You two can turn around and ride but I'm going on.'

Black leaned across to Hart. 'We

must be closer to San Remo than we are to Apache Hills, Tom. It makes sense to carry on.'

Jim Welch squinted at the trail ahead of them as the sun began to slowly disappear into it. Darkness was now spreading quickly across the three riders and he knew that he had to make a decision.

'You figure we can keep on this road through the night?' Black and Hart grunted at the man in unison.

Welch slapped his reins and started towards the setting sun with his cohorts in close pursuit. He was not about to make camp out here in this deadly place even if it got so dark that he had to walk his horse. San Remo was somewhere ahead. That at least was known.

Kid Palomino and Red Rivers were also out there unless they had perished in the desert off to the left of the bone-dry trail. That was also a fact, Welch thought as he rode on.

But the shots had come from their

right. He was sure of that too. That meant someone else was roaming around in this parched country. Someone who was armed.

As the three men drove their horses towards the glowing western sky, they knew darkness offered them no answers.

It also offered them little or no protection.

★　★　★

Blue Snow had stopped his pony as soon as he too heard the chilling shots ringing out far ahead of them in the prairie which he knew lay beyond the desert. Kid Palomino and Red Rivers had sat in their saddles a few paces behind the silent Comanche, waiting to see what the warrior would do next.

For more than five minutes Blue Snow simply looked around at the dunes which encircled them. His face was like a carved stone statue, unwilling or unable to show any emotion. Whatever he was thinking or feeling was hidden from the two men he had saved back in the heart of the deadly desert of sand. Yet he continued looking around them as if trying to see something their eyes would never recognize.

Without turning to his companions, the warrior tapped his heels against the sides of his mount and started riding on once more.

The two lawmen drew level with the Comanche and tried to see signs of emotion on his face as the last rays of the sun illuminated his chiselled features. There seemed to be none.

Palomino turned to Red Rivers as they cantered on.

'We must be getting close to something or someone, Red.'

'Sure enough. There has to be at least one varmint with a gun or carbine pretty close,' Rivers replied. He continued urging his horse on through the sand when they began to ascend yet another massive dune.

'What do you think, Blue Snow?' the Kid asked the quiet Indian as he steered his mount up the soft sand. 'Have you any ideas about who fired them shots?'

Blue Snow said nothing, he just held on to the mane of his pony until it reached the very top of the sand-dune. The sun was almost gone by the time the two Texan lawmen reached his side and stopped their horses. Before the light evaporated, revealing a thousand stars, their tired eyes caught a brief glimpse of the prairie and its strange vegetation.

Then darkness engulfed their view of everything which lay ahead of their three mounts.

Kid Palomino rested a hand on the shoulders of the two riders to either side of him and sighed thankfully. That glimpse of the tall Joshua trees and cactus told him that they had somehow managed to cross the deadly desert with the help of the strangely silent Comanche.

As the cold chill of night brushed across them, reminding the three horsemen that their plight was not yet at an end, Kid Palomino looked at Red Rivers, whose craggy features were bathed in starlight.

'I don't see no lights anywhere. Do you?'

'Nope. San Remo must still be a long ways off,' Red answered. He searched his vest pockets for his trusty tobacco-pouch and matches. For the first time in over three days, he felt like making a cigarette.

'There's enough brush down there for us to make a camp-fire tonight, Red,' Palomino said cheerfully.

'No make fire,' Blue Snow said forcefully.

'Why not, Blue Snow?' Red asked. He licked the gummed paper of his smoke.

'No smoke either,' the Comanche said, grabbing the cigarette from Red Rivers and tossing it to the ground.

'What's wrong, *amigo*?' Kid Palomino

reached across and touched the arm of the Indian.

'Evil out there, Kid,' Blue Snow replied.

Both lawmen knew they had heard fear in the voice of the Comanche. If whatever was out there could scare Blue Snow, they knew it must be something worthy of respect.

Suddenly they, too, were frightened.

12

They were the remnants of another time, another age. The dregs of a society which now shunned them for the things they had done and continued to do. These were not men who deserved to be called by the name. They had been called animals by many but no animal could or would stoop as low as these riders.

They had become exiles from civilization itself. None was worthy of ever being accepted back into a normal world. Yet it did not seem to matter to any of them as they ploughed on through the dense prairie astride their exhausted horses.

They had to continue on, doing as they had done for so many years during and since the war; never even thinking about the effects their acts of carnage had upon the innocent victims who endured the atrocities.

None of the riders who drove their mounts on through the darkness belonged in this or any other civilized world, but they were still here. They had relinquished any right to being considered anything but vermin long ago, but they were still here.

They still wore the heavy grey uniforms of a defeated army but these men were defeated neither in spirit nor resolve. Now a mere haunting of what they must have once been when it all began so long ago, the riders rode on, screaming out their battle cry whenever they felt the last traces of guilt creeping into what remained of their souls.

The South would rise again.

They had been telling themselves that since they had first found out their side had lost the war. The Union forces could not have beaten these men even if Lee had capitulated. They would never ever lower the tattered and torn standard which they flew proudly.

The were the last of the Confederate forces.

Still seeking a place to create their new world, they rode on destroying all which lay in their way. Never truly believing that their once great army had been defeated, they drove on from one atrocity to the next.

Each day allowed them to continue their brutal crusade.

And only one man seemed capable of controlling them. His name was Zeb Coltrane, the most deadly and despicable of them all.

Zeb Coltrane ruled his fifty followers with a strength born out of the desperation only a man unwilling ever to bow his head to another could muster. He simply had to reign over his men like a medieval tyrant. There was no other way to survive, and he knew it.

There had once been more than a hundred and fifty men in his ruthless army of followers, but one by one they had been whittled away. Yet there were still more than enough riders for him to overwhelm any town which stood in their way. More than enough deadly killers to destroy all who dared challenge them.

Coltrane's Raiders had managed to ravage their way through what remained of the Southern states before even their own supporters turned against them. They had raped and looted and destroyed more of the once proud Southern states than the Union forces but had never had even a twinge of regret or conscience.

For only real men cared.

It had been a long time since any of Coltrane's Raiders had been real men.

Forced to move further and further west, the riders found themselves in the territory of New Mexico and knew there were rich pickings to be found in this large land; a land where the law was barely noticeable.

Coltrane led his men on and on from one killing spree to the next. Never staying in one spot long enough for anyone to catch their putrid scent, the self-styled leader drove his army ever onward, seeking a place that he might be able to claim as his own.

Some men seek to be King.

Zeb Coltrane was such a man. He knew that this territory was so big that there had to be a place that he could claim for himself and his followers. He would raise their tattered flag and pronounce himself ruler.

But this was a land which the various tribes of Indians had been forced to occupy, as their own lands had fallen into the hands of the ever-expanding America.

So many Indians that they had proved to be a nuisance to Coltrane and his followers. Having had no conscience about killing white people of any age or sex, the rebel leader did not think twice about killing men of a darker skin. The venom that they had once unleashed on their slaves, they now inflicted mercilessly on the poor unsuspecting red-skinned natives.

Even the experienced Comanche

were no match for the pure evil of Zeb Coltrane's Raiders. They had fallen, as all others had fallen before them, at the hands of the dirtiest fighters ever to enter this once peaceful territory.

Coltrane's was a plan of almost Biblical enormity. If he had to kill every man, woman and child in New Mexico to achieve it, he would. Most white people on remote farms had little, so he just killed them and left their bodies to feed the buzzards. But killing Indians was a different matter.

Most of those victims wore jewellery of gold and silver. They placed no value upon these trinkets, but Coltrane did. He would execute all the Indians he came across and have their bodies buried in shallow graves which he marked on a crude map he kept on his person at all times. When the time was right, he would lead his army back, to all the places where he had left the corpses and retrieve the fortune they had around their necks and wrists.

He was accumulating his own hidden

fortune. A treasure-trove that he would use later, when he required funds to fulfil his ambitious plans.

Immediate wealth came from the towns he had razed to the ground. Towns had banks and lots of people who had money. After relieving these people of their money, he would simply have them all killed and then leave nothing but ashes as he led his riders on to the next town. It was an effective plan.

Zeb Coltrane held no title as did others who had fought valiantly during the war. Yet he was the undisputed leader of the wild band. He ruled his followers through cunning and brutal force. As he led the fifty riders through the dark prairie toward his next goal, he knew none would ever raise a finger against him. Their spirits had been crushed long ago.

Whatever he said, they did.

Zeb Coltrane rode at the head of his Raiders on towards San Remo simply because it was there. Another ripe fruit waiting to be plucked from life itself. By the time Coltrane was finished, it would be yet another burning memory. Another town wiped off the map for good.

If anyone in San Remo had known what was heading in their direction, they would have fled for their lives.

The trouble was, they did not know.

★   ★   ★

Major Joseph Saunders and his men had proceeded with far more caution than usual as they made their way up through the vicious prairie brush towards the top of the butte. It had been more than two hours since the major and his thirty weary troopers had heard the pair of echoing shots. Darkness offered the single-file line of cavalry little protection as they quietly allowed their horses to walk toward the distant peak. They knew that at any time they might suddenly be ripped apart by the bullets of those who had executed the eighteen Indians and left the bodies in shallow graves far behind them.

It was as if the troopers' mounts knew of the danger which might be surrounding them as they silently walked up towards the sand covered summit. None had made the slightest noise for the duration of the long trek.

Saunders had noticed one thing immediately he had started up toward where they had heard the two chilling shots. The brush, which was impregnable for the most part, had been beaten into submission by whoever had come this way before them. There was a wide clear route up to the top of the butte. As Major Saunders led his small force ever upward, by the light of the stars, he knew they were tracking a much larger body of men.

The major seemed to know instinctively that he was in close pursuit of an army. Or what was left of one.

His blood had chilled in his veins as his keen eyes first noticed the sabre cuts on the cactus and Joshua trees. A trail had been carved out for a large group of riders, by men who knew how to handle razor-sharp swords.

Saunders knew that only one other body of men apart from the Union soldiers trained their men to use such lethal weaponry. The Confederates.

Yet the war had ended a long time ago.

Joseph Saunders knew that meant only one thing. They were on the trail of renegades. Confederate rebels who, unlike Jesse and Frank James, had not turned to crime, but remained what they had been taught to be.

Cold-blooded killing machines.

As the thirty troopers finally reached the flat top of the butte they were commanded to dismount by the anxious officer. Saunders walked around the scene with a silence that troubled his men. Even Sergeant Dean was worried by what they had found.

There had been no attempt to disguise the fact that at least fifty men had camped here for probably more than a week. The grim-faced major could not conceal his worry as he walked around the litter that only men can create by their mere existence.

'Major,' one of the troopers said as he knelt beside a pile of ashes.

Saunders turned and stared.

'This is still warm.' The young man began to stroke the ashes with his hand until sparks drifted into the dark sky above them. 'Whoever was camped here, only just left.'

'I thought as much,' Saunders said. He walked towards the men who were gathered around the kneeling trooper.

'Looks like a lot of men were here, sir,' Sergeant Dean growled, kicking an empty can across the churned-up ground.

'They must have been here for quite some time,' Saunders said. His eyes vainly searched the area for signs of his two Crow scouts.

'Look, sir.' Bruno Dean pointed at a mound of sand close to the fire.

Major Saunders aimed his boots at the place towards which Bruno Dean was already walking. Both soldiers knew what lay beneath the sand but they still felt compelled to kneel down and claw away at the fluid grains. As before, they found what they were looking for a mere few inches below the surface of the sand.

It took only seconds for them to uncover the faces of Rooster and Smiling Joe, their Crow scouts. Both were staring with dead eyes up at the stars.

'Reckon they never seen what hit them,' Saunders said as he felt the blood underneath Rooster's head. He could feel the bullet hole in the base of the Indian's skull. 'They were both executed in exactly the same way as the Apache and Comanche Indians we found earlier.'

'Who are we chasing, Major?' Bruno Dean asked in a whispered tone intended to reach only the officer's ears. 'Who the hell are we chasing?'

'Rebels, Sergeant,' Saunders responded quietly. He stood up. 'We're chasing a mighty big bunch of rebels.'

'Maybe now we ought to turn back for Fort Grant,' Sergeant Dean suggested as he walked beside the officer, heading towards the waiting troopers.

Saunders gazed around the faces of his men.

'Make camp, men. Rekindle that fire.'

Bruno Dean waved his hands at the soldiers and turned around to face the determined major.

'But what if them Rebs come back?'

'They won't,' Joseph Saunders said. He sighed as he gazed out at the blackness below them. It was obvious why the large force of rebels had used this for their camp, he thought. Although only about fifty feet higher than the land around them, it gave unlimited views in every direction. From here, a skilled officer and a handful of riflemen could hold off an entire army for ever.

'Are you sure they ain't gonna come

back, sir?' the burly sergeant asked.

Saunders gritted his teeth and pointed.

'They went down through there, Dean. That's slow and heavy going by anyone's standards. But they've got sabres to hack a trail out where none existed previously.'

Bruno Dean scratched his unshaven chin.

'Which gives us time to have us a meal.'

'Exactly.' Saunders patted the man on his shoulder. 'Let them do all the hard work forging a way through that devilish brush, while we rest up and fill our bellies. Come daybreak, we'll use the ready-made trail to catch up with them. We'll be fresh and they'll be dog tired.'

'What if they decide to make a fight of it, sir?' Dean swallowed hard.

'I'm praying they do, Sergeant Dean. Then we can teach them a lesson they'll never forget.'

Dean nodded. He watched the men

eagerly making camp behind them. The fire came to life again as dry kindling was piled on to the still-hot ashes. As the sergeant walked towards the busy troopers leaving the officer staring into the darkness below he knew that, for some of them, this would be their final night on earth.

13

San Remo was prosperous by New Mexico standards, yet about as far away from civilization as it was possible to get without falling off the very edge of the world into hell itself. For all its wealth it stood alone amid the cactus and sagebrush of the prairie, defiant and confident.

Sheriff Ned Romero had been in office for two years and knew he would win a second term because no sane man wanted the job he had so cherished.

For even here where nothing seemed to ever happen to rouse the sleeping residents out of their complacency, being a lawman was something some-one else did. Lawmen cleaned up the mess left by others and dared to face the unknown with only a tin star pinned to their vests.

Romero was, as his name implied, a man of Latin origin yet he seemed to prize the thought of one day becoming an American more than most. He had arrived in San Remo many years earlier with only the clothes he wore on his back. He had cleaned out the stables and done every job he could get in order to feed his wife and numerous offspring. There was no job too dirty for a man such as Romero.

He had worked his way into the hearts of all who lived in the quiet remote town simply because of his hard work and endeavour. When the old sheriff had retired two summers earlier Romero stood for the post unopposed.

Sheriff Ned Romero had wired far and wide trying to find two deputies who could take the pressure off himself and allow him a little free time with his family. Twenty-four hours' duty a day was more than even he was used to, but there seemed to be no takers.

For nearly twelve months he heard nothing. It was as if, unlike himself, nobody wanted to visit the distant town where people died of boredom and very little else.

Then, when the weary sheriff thought he would never manage to persuade anyone to take up the posts of deputies, he received a reply.

Kid Palomino and his partner Red Rivers had heard of the deputy jobs and decided to leave the comfort of their Texas homeland and ride to a territory they had never visited before.

To them, it was just another adventure to add to the catalogue of previous ones. Something which would pass a little time until they felt the urge to move on. They had roamed the West, working mostly as lawmen, and had earned the reputation that was branded permanently on their names.

When Romero had first received the wire from the Kid and Rivers, he had been elated. But that had been over three weeks earlier and he had not heard anything since. The sheriff was becoming anxious. Had they changed their minds or had a better offer? Perhaps they had met with an accident. Whatever the reason for their delay in reaching San Remo, it was now of great concern to the sheriff.

Standing on the porch of his office, bathed in lantern light, Ned Romero sucked on a long cigar as he watched the trail which led straight into his town. A dozen lights from a dozen façades spilled their illumination across the dark thoroughfare, yielding no answers to the thoughtful lawman.

Romero had tried to send another message that very afternoon but the old man in the weathered telegraph office had told him that the wires were dead.

As smoke drifted from beneath his proud black moustache, Ned Romero knew something was wrong. For the first time in all the years he had lived in San Remo, he was actually worried.

Worried about what was out there in the darkness.

It was an irrational fear considering the town's peaceful history but the sheriff was unable to rid his mind of the thoughts which buzzed like hornets in his fertile brain. Had the time finally arrived when he would be required to earn his salary and become a true law-officer?

The thought troubled him.

He was no coward: there were few braver, but he had never been required to prove himself in the eyes of the residents of San Remo. Would he be able to cut the mustard if the time came?

A stream of questions flooded through his mind. Doubts where none had previously existed, raised their heads and mocked him as he inhaled the strong smoke of the long cigar.

Why was the telegraph office unable to send or receive wires? Why had Kid Palomino and Red Rivers not arrived in San Remo yet? So many questions and so few answers.

For the first time since he had taken office as the sheriff of this insignificant town, Romero was wearing a sidearm.

He had strapped on the gunbelt which came with the job and checked the Colt Peacemaker twice before sliding it into its leather resting place.

For the first time he was armed as he went through his nightly duties of checking the dozens of adobe buildings. As he paced silently between the buildings checking that all the doors were locked, Ned Romero felt sweat trickling down his face from beneath his straw hat.

He was worried and yet had no idea why.

Had the evil scent of what was heading towards his beloved town been caught in his keen nostrils? Whatever was alerting the sheriff to the impending dangers, it was very real.

Ned Romero walked slowly towards the edge of his town and rested an arm on the top fence-pole of the livery stables. He listened. He could hear something approaching out there in the dark prairie. His hand rested on the unfamiliar grip of his Colt.

As the sound grew louder, the sheriff walked on until he found a shadow big enough to protect him from the lights of the various buildings around him.

As he felt the pistol in the palm of his sweating hand, his eyes caught a glimpse of three riders in the light of a thousand stars, heading out of the prairie towards him.

Without even thinking, Romero thumbed back the hammer of his gun until it was fully locked. He waited. With each beat of his pounding heart, he could see the images growing closer and closer.

There were three of them, he thought.

Three riders allowing their mounts to find their own pace as they reached the boundaries of San Remo.

Ned Romero stepped out from the shadows, held his pistol at arm's length and shouted loudly at the riders:

'Stop right there, strangers. Stop or I'll fire.'

All three riders did exactly as the sheriff had commanded and reined in their horses. As the dust cleared, Romero found himself facing three men of very different aspects.

14

The sheriff's eyes were screwed up tightly as he peered into the faces of the three riders. These did not look like the sort of visitors he had expected to see. The lantern lights from the buildings around them illuminated the trio of horsemen and bathed them in an orange glow as they sat astride their snorting mounts.

Ned Romero was curious.

'You must be Sheriff Romero,' Kid Palomino said with a broad smile across his dusty face.

'Howdy, Ned,' Red grinned from behind the mask of trail-dust which caked his bearded features.

Sheriff Romero suddenly felt a weight being lifted off his troubled shoulders as he recognized the famous stallion beneath the grinning Kid Palomino. The lawman had heard many tales about the magnificent horse and his tired eyes told him the stories were all true.

'You must be Kid Palomino,' Romero said. He stepped closer to the head of the handsome animal and ran a hand down its long neck.

'Yep. That's what they call me,' the Kid replied. He slid off his tall mount and shook Romero's hand. 'I'm sorry we're kinda late getting here.'

Romero holstered his Peacemaker.

'I thought there was only going to be two of you,' he observed, staring up at the silent Comanche warrior sitting on his pony next to Red Rivers. 'I see you picked up a travelling companion somewhere along the way. How come?'

'There were only two of us when we set out, but we nearly got ourselves killed out in that desert. Without Blue Snow here, we'd have been buzzard-bait by now,' Kid Palomino explained. 'He saved our lives.'

'Blue Snow? That name's kinda familiar,' said Romero. He looked up at the stony-faced Indian.

The Comanche said nothing.

Red Rivers dismounted and patted the sheriff on his back.

'Don't you go worrying none about old Blue Snow, Ned. He's a real good Comanche and me and Palomino owe him our lives.'

Kid Palomino gathered up his reins in his gloved hands and thoughtfully studied the sheriff.

'Somewhere out in that prairie there must be a mighty big bunch of hardened killers, Sheriff,' he told Romero.

'How do you come by that notion?' Romero asked.

'Because Blue Snow was part of a hunting-party and although he won't spill the beans, someone killed them all,' Kid Palomino said. 'I reckon he must have escaped by the skin of his teeth, but he ain't much of a talker.'

'I've had me a gut feeling that there was someone out there in the prairie, Kid,' Ned Romero confessed. 'I guess you just confirmed my worst fears.'

'They must be a pretty useful bunch to kill Comanche in cold blood, Ned,' Red said, stroking the dust from his faithful horse. 'It takes a lotta skill to get the better even of drunk Comanche, let alone sober ones.'

'There are a lot of folks around here who don't give a damn what happens to Indians, boys,' the sheriff admitted regretfully.

'Are you one of those folks, Sheriff?' Kid Palomino stared hard at the face of the law officer.

'Nope. I ain't one of those kinda folks, Kid. I figure a man is a man whatever his skin colour.' Ned Romero ran a finger along his black moustache.

The Kid grinned again.

'Good. Because if'n you was that sort, I don't think I could work as your deputy.'

'Me neither,' Red added.

'You boys want some vittles?' the sheriff asked. 'I got me some chilli on the stove in the office. Should be just about ready by now.'

Kid Palomino grinned even wider and nodded up to the silent Blue Snow.

'Come on, my friend. We are going to have us some supper.'

Blue Snow held on to the mane of his highly decorated pony and shook his head slowly.

'You safe now with own kind. Me go.'

Before Kid Palomino or Red Rivers could utter another word, the Indian had turned his pony and galloped off into the dark prairie. Both men stood side by side in disbelief. The sheriff stepped between them.

'He's probably safer out there than here in San Remo. We've got some ornery critters who don't cotton to Indians of any description.'

'That might be an Indian but he's the best man me and Red here have ever had the luck to meet,' Palomino told the sheriff.

'I don't get it, Kid,' Red said as he stepped away from the two men who were watching the Comanche disappearing off into the night. 'How come he lit out like that?'

'Maybe he just don't like the smell of town folks,' The Kid said and smiled. He turned and began leading Nugget down the street.

Red Rivers sniffed the air.

'Yeah, there is a real bad smell around here, now you come to mention it.'

Palomino glanced across at Ned Romero and winked.

'Those are words coming from a man who can make a cake of soap last for ever, Sheriff.'

*   *   *

Jim Welch and his two companions had ridden for hours throughout the night along the seemingly endless trail which they were beginning to doubt would ever get them to San Remo. Twisting valleys full of tall Joshua trees and vicious cactus that seemed almost to

133

touch the stars above them, made the slow ride along the narrow trail road a nerve-racking ordeal.

When they reined in to water their mounts for the third time since they had started out from Apache Hills the three men wondered whether they would ever find the town they so desperately sought.

Welch left the tedious chore of watering the animals to Black and walked away from the steaming horses with Tom Hart at his elbow.

'This ain't going to plan,' Welch admitted angrily. He balled his fists as if to curse the darkness that had trapped them.

Hart was surprised by the outburst. It was the first time he had ever heard the older man admitting he just might have made a mistake.

'San Remo can't be far, Jim. We would probably be there by now if it weren't so dark.'

Welch nodded. He found the crumbling butt of a cigar in his coat-pocket and rammed it between his teeth.

'Yeah, if it were light, we could have let the horses have their heads, but it's too damn dark. Too dangerous. This road has a million potholes waiting for our horses to snap a leg in.'

'We must be darn close. We have to be.'

'I wonder if Kid Palomino made it across that desert, Tom.'

'His sort are lucky,' Hart spat.

'Until I catch up with him.' Welch chuckled to himself as he thought of the thousand ways he could kill the famed lawman. 'I'm gonna kill him slow. So slow he'll be begging for me to end his life.'

Tom Hart looked up at the sky.

'Pity there ain't a moon. A good moon can be as useful as the sun for seeing things.'

Suddenly there was a noise away in the prairie to the right of the three men.

'What was that?' Hart asked. Welch spat out the cigar butt and turned away.

Jim Welch did not answer, but ran

hurriedly back to where their horses were drinking. He pulled his carbine out of its saddle scabbard. Without a second's hesitation he had cranked its mechanism. He tried to see where the sound was coming from as Tom Hart and Ben Black followed his example. Welch turned as his keen ears began to tell him that whoever was moving through the brush was heading to a point a hundred yards or so behind them.

'You see anything, Jim?' Black asked. He knelt down and studied the dense undergrowth in front of them.

'Hush up, boy,' Welch ordered. He stepped forward cautiously, trying to see what was making so much noise.

The sound was growing louder with every passing second. It was not a sound any of the three outlaws liked.

It was riders. A lot of riders all heading towards the trail behind them.

Jim Welch turned quickly on his heels and moved back to the other men.

'I reckon there are dozens of riders moving through that cactus patch, boys. They sound as if they're heading this way.' Ben Black rose to his full height and stared out into the black shadows which loomed above them like creatures from another world.

'A posse? Could it be a posse, Jim?'

'Not likely,' Welch whispered as he held his Winchester firmly in his hands and tried to see something he might aim at. 'Even a posse wouldn't be crazy enough to ride through that sort of ground. Whoever they are, they ain't the law.'

'Then who?' Hart's voice was breaking again as it always did whenever they were faced with things they neither knew nor understood. 'Who do you figure it is?'

Welch grabbed the shoulder of the younger man and pushed him towards his horse. He gathered up his own reins.

'Could be the varmints who let loose with them two shots earlier tonight.'

Ben Black felt sweat pouring down his back beneath his shirt as he stepped forward.

'But who are they?'

'Whoever they are, I figure we don't wanna meet them out here, boys.' Welch reached for his saddle horn and dragged himself back on top of his horse. He slid the repeating rifle back into its leather scabbard beneath the saddle. 'Come on.'

The two outlaws hurriedly mounted their own horses. They heard the sound of noisy riders breaking through the last of the brush behind them.

'Look, Jim. Look.' Tom Hart pointed behind them down the trail. Flashing sabres were hacking at the last of the dense undergrowth as they found the trail.

'Ride, boys. Ride for your lives,' Welch yelled to Hart and Black. He spurred his horse and led his two young cohorts along the dark dusty trail, away from their unexpected visitors.

For the first time since sunset the

three outlaws were thankful that darkness was now protecting them from being seen.

They rode their horses up and over a rise and galloped down the other side. They knew they had not been spotted by whoever it was who had forced their mounts through the seemingly impenetrable prairie. If they had been seen, it would have been impossible for them to have outridden the hail of lethal lead that would have rained down on them.

Riding as if fleeing the Grim Reaper himself, the three outlaws forged on down the almost straight trail until they came to another small hill. With only the light of countless stars to guide them, they reached the top of the hill and then spotted something a few miles ahead.

The twinkling glow of amber lantern-lights stood out like fireflies amid the darkness. At last they had found it.

The three men thundered on towards San Remo.

15

Kid Palomino had only just dipped his spoon into the bowl of hot aromatic chilli when he and his two companions heard the sound of horses' hoofs thundering into the streets of San Remo. Palomino's eyes flashed up at Red Rivers and then the sheriff who was sitting at the large desk inside the office.

'Riders!' the Kid exclaimed. He left his food on top of a chest of drawers and walked to the open doorway of the sheriff's office. He stared down the street.

'Is everything OK?' Romero asked, patting a napkin against his mouth.

'What ya see, Palomino?' Red Rivers asked. He dragged himself out of the comfortable chair and made his way to the side of his tall friend.

Palomino stood watching the three

riders who quickly dismounted outside the livery and started hammering on the locked stable doors with their fists.

'Three mighty troubled riders. Do you know them, Sheriff?'

Ned Romero walked around the table and up to his two newly appointed deputies. He gazed down at the three noisy men who seemed desperate to awaken the owner of the stables.

'Nope, Kid. I ain't ever set eyes on them before.'

Palomino bit his lower lip thoughtfully. There were only three of them. They could not be connected with the killing of Blue Snow's fellow Comanche warriors. Or could they?

'Something must have sure spooked them *hombres*.'

'Yeah, but what?' Red rubbed the chilli off his mouth across the back of his sleeve.

Kid Palomino instinctively checked his pair of pearl-handled Colts and stepped out on to the porch.

'I reckon I'll go and find out.'

'Wait!' Romero said. He rushed to his desk and pulled open the top drawer. He picked up two gleaming tin stars and returned to the two men. 'I figure you ought to put these on.'

Both men did so willingly.

'Now they've got a target to aim at, Sheriff,' said Kid Palomino, and smiled as he walked along the porch with Red Rivers at his side and Ned Romero trailing a few paces behind. 'I ain't seen grown men act so scared before.'

'I wonder who they are,' Sheriff Romero pondered as he tried to keep pace with his deputies.

'I wonder *what* they are, Ned.' Red spat at the ground. 'They are pretty well-heeled for cowboys.'

'They ain't cowboys, Red,' Kid Palomino said bluntly.

'They can't be the critters who killed Blue Snow's pals,' Red opined as he checked his pistol.

'Whoever they are, they're sure scared,' the Kid observed. They stepped down on to the dusty street and continued towards the stables. 'I want to know why they're scared.'

By the time Red and the Kid had reached the corral fence, Ned Romero had caught up with his deputies.

'Easy, boys. I don't want to lose either of you to a stray bullet, not when I've waited so long for you to get here.'

'Stop fretting. I'm not in the mood to get shot, Sheriff,' Kid Palomino whispered over his shoulder.

Jim Welch was about to hit the locked door again when he saw the three approaching men. Their stars glinted in the light of the lanterns. Gesturing to Tom Hart and Ben Black he turned to face the walking men.

'Why all the damn noise, strangers?' Sheriff Ned Romero asked as he and his deputies stopped walking a mere ten feet from the waiting outlaws. 'You're making enough noise to wake the dead. How come?'

Welch stepped slightly ahead of his men and stared hard at the young deputy who towered over the other two men. He knew this had to be the man who had almost single-handedly killed his brother Hoyt and the rest of their gang back in Juárez. This had to be the famous Kid Palomino.

'There are riders back on the trail,' Jim Welch said, trying not to look at Kid Palomino with too much interest. He suddenly realized that if the massive sabre-wielding force was heading to San Remo, someone like Kid Palomino might just mean the difference between living and dying.

'The trail has always got riders on it, boys,' Sheriff Romero said, trying to work out why these three strangers were so terrified. They looked the sort that did not buckle under the weight of fear easily. Yet they were frightened. Every bead of sweat which glistened on their faces proved that.

'I mean, there are a lot of riders on the trail,' Welch explained. He glanced back at Hart and Black. 'I don't figure they're coming here for the sake of their health.'

'You boys look real scared,' Red Rivers said. 'How come?'

'Them riders came out of the prairie swinging sabres, mister,' Hart told him.

'Sabres?' Kid Palomino repeated the word.

'Who in tarnation carries sabres?' Ned Romero asked the tall Kid.

'Nobody I've ever heard of except troopers,' Palomino said thoughtfully. 'Are you sure it wasn't soldiers?'

'They looked like ghosts. All in grey,' Ben Black blurted out fearfully.

'No wonder you boys look a tad scared,' Red commented. He scratched his beard. 'Reckon *I*'d hightail it away from some varmint swinging a sword.'

'Men dressed in grey?' Kid Palomino murmured, glancing at the sheriff.

'There were dozens of them,' Welch added. 'We busted a gut riding here to warn you folks. It stands to reason that a bunch of riders that big are coming here for only one reason.'

'Sounds like renegade Confederates to me, Sheriff,' Palomino said. 'These boys could be right. They might be coming here to take San Remo by force.'

Ned Romero nodded.

'Sounds a fair bet, Kid.'

Jim Welch felt the hairs on his neck rise as he heard the sheriff call the tall deputy by name.

'So you are the famous Kid Palomino!'

'Yep. That's what they call me, stranger. Who might you be?'

Welch cleared his throat as his brain raced.

'The name's Jim. Jim Jones.'

'Nice to meet you, Mr Jones.' Palomino touched the brim of his white Stetson. He knew the name was probably false but there were other things to worry about far more important than a name.

'I thank you for warning us, boys. You want some supper?' the sheriff asked.

'Thanks, Sheriff. Me and the boys could use some grub before that bunch get here.'

Jim Welch signalled to his men and they followed the three lawmen towards the open doorway of the sheriff's office a few hundred yards away.

Kid Palomino walked with his head turned so he could watch the trio of strangers. For some reason, he did not trust any of them even though they had apparently come to warn San Remo of an impeding catastrophe.

'Where you boys headed?' the Kid asked as they all stepped up on to the wooden boardwalk outside the sheriff's office.

Welch paused as the rest of the men entered and looked straight into the eyes of the tall handsome deputy.

'Nowhere special.'

Kid Palomino nodded. He let the outlaw enter the office first. He knew the face of the man but could not recall where he had seen it before.

'We'd better wake up the town and get every able-bodied man ready, Sheriff,' the Kid suggested.

Ned Romero rubbed his chin.

'Good thinking, Kid. There must be at least twenty men with weapons in town.'

Red Rivers eyed up the strangers then stepped beside the sheriff.

'I'll tag along with you, Ned. We had better get them folks up fast. There's no telling how soon them critters will take to get here.'

As Romero and Red rushed to the first house, Kid Palomino stood silently in the doorframe watching the three strangers eating. He himself had lost his appetite.

16

They appeared with the rising sun on their backs. A line of sabre-wielding men with a single aim: to loot, kill and then destroy San Remo. They had travelled hundreds of miles doing exactly the same thing, so many times over so many years, that they had long forgotten why.

It had become the way they lived, and others died. A bloody ritual which had enabled what remained of the once mighty rebel force to survive. Yet it had proved a costly exercise, as Coltrane's dwindling army bore witness.

For each town they attacked saw his followers diminish in numbers. Unlike most outlaw gangs, it was impossible to recruit new men to replace the ones lost. For his men were of a different place and a different time.

Coltrane had no feelings either good

149

or bad for the town which lay before his men in the morning light. It was merely another obstacle to be taken and destroyed like all the others which had gone before it.

San Remo was simply the next town which stood in their way as they continued on towards their destiny. A few seconds after daybreak, Zeb Coltrane rode at the head of his fifty strong men along the narrow trail.

The riders were weary, yet refused to pause for even a moment as they rode slowly in the direction of the town of adobe buildings.

They had destroyed so many towns and so many people, so many, many times, they felt that they could take San Remo with their eyes closed.

On any other morning of any other day, that might just have been so. But not this morning. On this new day, there were no innocent citizens sleeping in their beds, blissfully unaware of what was arriving with the rising sun. Today, the people of San Remo were waiting.

Kid Palomino had used what had been left of the dark night to ensure that San Remo was ready for the inevitable attack. He had managed to get hold of every single buckboard the small town possessed and had blocked the main street at its half-way point.

Water-barrels and even furniture filled up the gaps between the upturned wooden vehicles and armed men waited with their rifles cocked behind the hastily constructed barricade.

The experienced deputy had placed armed men on the rooftops of every building along the main street. Now, as the sun bounced off the sabres of the rebel force riding slowly towards the town, he rested against the wall of the sheriff's office where Red Rivers and Ned Romero chewed on unlighted cigars.

Jim Welch and his two cohorts had done everything asked of them and were stationed right in the middle of the barricade with their arsenal of various weapons and ammunition at their feet.

'Here they come, Kid,' Romero said. His throat seemed unwilling to allow the words to pass his dry cracked lips.

Kid Palomino flipped the small leather safety-loops off his guns and flexed his fingers as he looked down towards the riders who were approaching silently. How many times had they done this, he pondered. Did they always strike at dawn? It made sense to attack when nearly every living soul was still asleep.

'How many do you count, Red?'

'Forty or fifty, Kid. It ain't easy to be certain,' Red Rivers replied, holding his trusty Colt in his shaking hand.

'Not with the sun behind them,' the sheriff added. He held a hand to his eyes, trying to see almost directly into the sun which was still low in the blue cloudless sky.

Kid Palomino looked hard at the distant riders. They did appear like ghosts, he thought. Their grey sun-bleached clothing, which had once been honourable uniforms, now hung on their wretched bodies like rags.

The Kid swallowed hard as he looked into the eyes of the troubled sheriff.

'Is everyone in their places, Ned?'

Romero nodded.

Red Rivers leaned towards his friend and whispered. For nearly a minute the red-haired man spoke quietly to his partner. When he was finished he stepped back and waited for a response.

'You're dead right, Red. Those three strangers are troubling me as much as they are you,' Palomino admitted. He cast an eye towards the centre of the street.

'I'll keep an eye on them,' Red said. He stepped down off the porch and walked across the wide street.

'Where are our horses?' Palomino called.

Red pointed to the far end of the

street, far away from the advancing rebels.

'Derby and Nugget are safe.'

Kid Palomino moved closer to Romero and placed a hand on the shoulder of the sweating man. He knew this was a good man. A man who did not deserve to be faced with this sort of horror.

'If you stay calm, everything will work out, Ned.'

'I have to tell you something. Something very important. I'm not much of a shot, Kid,' the sheriff confessed. He stared out at the dust which rose from the hoofs of the riders' horses who were now getting close to the boundaries of San Remo. 'I never have been much of a shot. I'm scared that I'll let you and Red down when the fighting starts.'

Palomino squeezed the man's shoulder, then turned and entered the office for a moment or two. As he walked back out on to the sun-bathed porch he handed a scatter gun and box of shells to the sheriff.

'Use this. It takes away the need for accuracy.'

Romero felt a smile crossing his face.

'Thanks, *amigo*.'

Suddenly it happened. Within the blinking of an eye, all hell broke loose in the main street of San Remo. The renegade leader, Zeb Coltrane had seen the sun bouncing off the rifle barrels poking over the makeshift barricade but was unafraid. He had also noticed the activity on the rooftops as inexperienced men tried to train their carbines down on his advancing renegade force.

Yet for some reason Coltrane did not see the danger, only the challenge. Or perhaps he did see it, but refused to acknowledge it.

Whatever the reason for Zeb Coltrane's rebel call as he stood in his stirrups and wielded his mighty sabre over his head, it chilled the citizens of San Remo, to a man. Coltrane almost seemed excited at the prospect of engaging in another fight, even though it might be his last.

Zeb Coltrane had made the sap rise in his battered warriors as he stood screaming at the sky. It was as if all fifty riders knew that for once, their victims were awake and armed. At long last they might be able to regain a fragment of their long lost dignity and actually do battle instead of simply slaughtering all who stood before them.

The people of San Remo had somehow found out about Coltrane's planned attack and were ready to defend themselves and the town of sunbaked buildings. They were actually waiting for the remnants of Coltrane's once great army with their rifles raised and primed.

Soon, every one of the ruthless army had joined their leader in yelling their battle cries at the heavens as they spurred on and on towards the waiting rifles.

Like bats out of Satan's lair, the screaming riders thundered straight into the main street of the isolated town. Their swords in one hand and reins in the other they charged at the men who hid behind the hastily built defences.

These riders were not easily frightened, for they had long ceased living like normal men. These were riders with the taste of blood from countless murders in their mouths.

They had come to silently slit the throats of every man jack of the people of San Remo, but now knew they had a fight on their hands.

A fight they actually relished.

If they had been any other group of riders, they would have changed their plans and given San Remo a wide berth. But not Zeb Coltrane or his followers. Perhaps they did not care any longer whether they lived or died on this hot sultry morning. Maybe they had journeyed too far on a trail they secretly wished had ended long ago back on the battlefields when honour had been their only companion.

Their horses gathered pace as they

charged. Men who had ridden towards Union cannons were unafraid of rifles. They drove their horses down into the wide dusty thoroughfare at breakneck speed toward the barricade as if defying the barrels of the deadly Winchesters that were aimed on them.

They rode as if in complete disdain of the men on top of the buildings which flanked the road, and of their bullets.

For all men there comes a day to face death. For Coltrane's Raiders, this was that day.

Kid Palomino had shouted at the top of his voice for the town's menfolk to open fire. Within seconds, all the armed men were firing their carbines. Bullets rained down from the high vantage-points on the buildings and spewed from every rifle at the manned barricade.

Seconds after Palomino had called out to the waiting people of San Remo to start shooting, the air was filled with the black stench of gunpowder.

Yet Coltrane's Raiders continued coming.

The Kid watched as men he had placed up on top of the buildings cocked and fired their Winchesters down at the yelling rebel riders.

Yet as he leaned against the wooden upright outside the sheriff's office, staring at the crazed grey-coated riders, his blood froze. As rider after rider was cut down, they still drove on fearlessly towards the barricade.

Were they insane?

There seemed to be not an ounce of fear in the riders who charged straight into the heart of the main street. They just kept coming and coming as bullets tore into their ranks.

As Kid Palomino ran along behind the men who were leaning against the barricade firing their rifles, he could hear the sound of the thunderous hoofs getting closer and closer.

Jim Welch watched as the tall deputy passed behind him and his two friends before he started shooting at the riders again. Before Palomino had reached the middle of the line of riflemen, the first of the horses leapt over the massive obstacles. Soon it was followed by another and then another.

The flashing razor-sharp blades of the riders swept down like sickles as they hacked at the terrified towns-people.

Using his expertise with his pair of Colts, Palomino dived to the ground, turned on to his back and started firing at the horses and riders who continued to leap over their high defences.

His deadly bullets found their mark, time after time, but the Kid saw his amateur army of riflemen being cut down. As he had claimed the fifth of the rebel riders, he could see that a similar number of his own people were lying either dead or dying. Some had been killed cleanly by the flashing blades whilst others lay searching for parts of their own bodies in the blood-soaked sand around them.

'Look out, Palomino,' Red Rivers'

voice yelled from above him as he saw three more riders forcing their horses through the very end of the barricade next to the cantina porch.

Swinging around and getting back on to his feet once more, the Kid fired into the gap. Suddenly he saw a sabre flying through the air towards him. Kid Palomino jumped back a few inches and felt the pain as its sharp blade sliced through the side of his right leg.

It felt like a thousand rattlers had sunk their fangs into his thigh.

With blood pouring from the wound, he saw one of the rebels riding straight at him. This had to be the man who had thrown his sabre, Palomino thought as he staggered sideways. The man was dragging his own pistol from its holster as he bore down on the tall limping deputy.

The Kid tried to turn and run for cover, his fingers squeezing the triggers of his matched guns. Both hammers fell on empty chambers while the rider got closer and closer. The horse snorted as

Palomino leapt across its forelegs whilst a bullet kicked up dust only inches from his trailing leg.

Palomino tried to run at the rider but felt his leg buckle beneath him as an agonizing pain exploded in the deep gash, sending him crashing into the sand as the rider turned his mount around again.

Suddenly, Kid Palomino saw the shadow of a man moving across the blood-soaked road. Looking up, he just caught a fleeting glimpse of Red Rivers as he dived from the balcony of a cantina straight on to the back of the shooting rider. The sheer impact of it as he hit the rider brought the horse down.

The sound of one of the rider's legs snapping as his mount rolled over seemed to echo off the walls of the adobe buildings before Red dispatched him with a single bullet.

Before the Kid could move, Red raised his pistol and fired twice more, bringing another pair of rebels off the backs of their mounts.

'Red!' Palomino shouted.

'Come on, Kid,' Red said. He ducked his head and shoulder under the younger man's arm and swooped him off into the cantina as bullets exploded all around them.

'You damn fool,' the Kid remonstrated, coughing. 'You're too old to jump off balconies.'

'I figured that just after I hit the ground, Kid.' Resting the bleeding Palomino on a hard chair, the red-whiskered man untied the knot in his partner's bandanna, dragged it from his neck and wrapped it around the leg-wound. He tied the knot as tightly as he could, then returned his attention to what was happening out in the street.

It was a blood-bath.

'This is crazy, Palomino. Damn crazy.'

'Got any ideas?' Kid Palomino shook the spent cartridges from his guns and then reloaded them. He had been in pain many times before in his life, but nothing like the pain he now endured. 'Right now, I'm open to any suggestions you can come up with, Red.'

'I got me a hankering to go back to Texas real bad at the moment.' Red Rivers ducked from the door to the window of the cantina and fired at the riders who were now trying to use the sheer weight of their horses to breach the barricade. It could be seen moving slowly as the rebels' mounts were driven at it. Coltrane and his men were now firing their arsenal of weaponry at the men above them. Screams rang out as one man after another fell heavily into the street.

'These townspeople are being picked off, Kid,' Red said as yet another man came crashing down off the roof to land in front of the door of the cantina.

'How many of them rebels are left, Red?' Palomino asked through gritted teeth as he managed to stand and limp to the window of the cantina. His pal fired another telling shot at their attackers.

Red's face was grim.

'Hard to say, Kid. I figure we must have done for maybe a quarter of them but they're picking off these townsfolk darn easy.'

Palomino glanced down at his leg and saw the blood spurting out from the deep gash.

'We have to stop them before it's too late.'

Red winced as he saw Tom Hart being crushed by a seventeen-hand sorrel which landed directly on top of him. Its master spurred the huge animal over the wooden barrels between two upturned buckboards.

'One of Jim Jones's men has just got himself killed.'

Palomino raised his left-hand gun and fired through the window at the rider. The bullet hit the man in his neck and sent his lifeless body tumbling into the rock-hard ground, his terrified mount bucking at everything around it. The Kid watched as the man he knew as Jim Jones used his Winchester to kill the horse before firing between the large bloody gap at the ruthless riders.

'This is bad, Kid,' Red said, sliding new bullets into the hot chambers of his pistol. 'These rebels are plumb loco. They just won't quit.'

Kid Palomino staggered to the side of his sidekick and gasped as he tried to force the pain from his body by sheer willpower.

'These folks are getting themselves slaughtered.'

'I know, but what can we do?' Red asked. He snapped the cylinder back into the body of his gun and then dragged its hammer into position with his thumb.

'Got any dynamite?' The Kid fired two more shots into the cloud of dust beyond the buck-boards before taking cover behind the wall next to the window.

'Not on me,' Red Rivers replied as a bullet took part of the door frame off the wall, a mere two inches above his battered hat. Dust and splinters showered over him as he tried to see who had fired the shot. It was hopeless. The street was thick with choking gunsmoke and dust, reducing visibility with every passing heartbeat.

'If we had a few sticks of dynamite, we could end this massacre right now,' Palomino said. Sweat was running freely down his face and along his square jaw.

Red nodded in agreement.

'I figure that only dynamite can stop them critters.'

'Reckon there is any dynamite in this town?' Kid Palomino rubbed the sweat off his face and listened to the rebel screams of Zeb Coltrane and his cohorts as they continued shooting and trying to force-down the town's meagre defences.

'Ned Romero would know,' Rivers said. He shook the dust from his Stetson and moved closer to the door. 'If there is a single stick in San Remo, he'd know.'

'Where is he?' The words had barely

left the lips of Kid Palomino when they heard the unmistakable sound of a shotgun being fired from above them. The sound of injured horses and riders chilled the deputies' blood.

'That must be him,' Palomino said pointing his gun upward.

'You give him the scattergun?'

'Seemed like a good idea at the time, Red.' Palomino accepted the hand of his partner as they both headed for the rear of the building. A flight of wooden steps situated just behind the huge ovens of the cantina, faced the pair.

It led directly to the upper floor and then on to the roof. As they ascended the stairwell, another thunderous blast echoed off the walls around them.

'You're bleeding bad, Palomino,' Red said as they reached the upper floor.

'No time to fret on that, Red.' Palomino limped quickly to the open windows which led to the balcony where the sheriff was kneeling with the smoking shotgun in his hands.

Ned Romero glanced at the two faces

inside the room.

'We've cut half of them down, boys.'

Red Rivers reached out, grabbed hold of the sheriff and dragged him inside the dark room. As Romero lay on his back still clutching on to the huge weapon, a volley of shots peppered the spot where he had been kneeling only a few seconds earlier.

'Damn!' Sheriff Romero exclaimed, rising slowly up from the floor. 'That was close.'

'Is there any dynamite in this town, Ned?' Kid Palomino asked.

Romero scratched his face.

'There might be some in the hardware store, I guess.'

'Come on, Ned. We gotta go and see,' Red said. He grabbed the sheriff's arm and led him to the door.

'Your leg,' Romero said to Palomino as he noticed the blood streaming down over the tall man's pants from the blood-soaked bandanna tied around his leg. 'You're wounded, Kid.'

'I'm OK. Go and show Red where

the hardware store is, Ned,' Palomino said calmly. 'We gotta stop this before these varmints kill everyone.'

'You sure that you're OK, Kid?' Red asked.

'Leave me your matches, Red,' Palomino said, holding his hand out to the bearded man.

Red tossed the box of matches to his pal without question, then turned and followed Romero.

Kid Palomino watched the sheriff leading Red down the stairs, then sat down on a chair as bullets smashed the glass out of the windows in the room. The Kid was losing too much blood and he knew it.

He pulled a bullet from his belt, placed its brass casing between his teeth and began to loosen it. The wounded deputy knew he had to do something fast in order to stop the bleeding.

As the lead ball was freed from the bullet, Palomino carefully held on to the brass casing so the gunpowder remained inside it as he untied the bandanna with his free hand.

He pulled at the torn pants where the sabre had sliced into his leg and wiped the blood away enough to sprinkle the gunpowder over the deep oozing cut.

The powder burned like hell as Kid Palomino gritted his teeth and fumbled with the box of matches. His fingers were sticky with blood as he managed to pull one of the inch-long lucifer sticks free of the box. Striking it, he dropped the flaming match on to the wound. A bright flash temporarily blinded the young deputy as he rocked back and forth on the chair in agony.

The smell of smouldering flesh filled his nostrils.

Through tear-filled eyes, Palomino saw the wound had stopped bleeding. Somehow he managed to stand and stagger to the window and look down on the raging battle; a battle San Remo was losing.

Then he noticed that the box of

matches was still in his hand. He leaned
against the wall, his eyes searching the
room until he saw what he was looking
for.

On a small dresser, he saw it.

17

Sheriff Ned Romero led Red Rivers to a narrow alley at the back of the buildings. For the two running men with tin stars pinned to their vests, this was an unnerving situation by anyone's standards. For the hardware store stood next to the livery stables near the edge of San Remo.

They knew that with every footstep they were actually moving behind the ruthless rebel riders. There was the faint possibility that if they did not find any dynamite in the deserted store, they could try and use their weapons to trap the savage horsemen at the barricade.

Neither man relished the thought.

They seemed to be running for an eternity, yet actually it had been only a matter of seconds, the sound of the raging battle echoing around them from the main street.

They had not spoken to one another since leaving the injured Kid Palomino up in the room above the cantina. There seemed to be no words which could truly express the sheer horror that both men felt in their hearts at what was occurring only a few dozen yards away from them.

Would they be able to find any precious sticks of dynamite in the store? The uncertainty racked both men. Both knew what they would have to do if they failed. To be forced to stand in the wide main street and attempt to cut down the riders from behind their ranks was tantamount to committing suicide, but sometimes that was what it took.

The prospect troubled them both.

Reaching the rear door of the hardware store, both men paused momentarily as they stared through the glass pane straight through the building. They could see the firing riders passing before the large front window quite clearly.

Taking a deep breath, Red Rivers

raised his right leg and kicked at the lock. It shattered beneath his Cuban heel and the door swung inward.

Ned Romero clutched the heavy shotgun across his chest as his deputy licked his dry lips until he was sure there was nobody else inside the dark interior.

'Come on,' Red whispered.

Moving cautiously through the array of counters, they searched for dynamite and fuses. Neither man had realized how much stock lay inside the average hardware store until this very moment. Shelves were bulging under the weight of everything from nails to roof-shingles. Glass-topped counters held knives of every shape and description, guns and parts for guns as well as ammunition of all calibres.

Rolls of chicken-wire were stacked next to barrels of pickaxe handles. The store was an Aladdin's cave with no beginning or end to its range of items.

'Do you figure there are any sticks of dynamite in this damn place, Ned?' Red asked as he moved around the shelves carefully so that none of Coltrane's men would catch a glimpse of him through the large window. The battle was still furiously refusing to end outside in the street as both men moved closer to one another.

The sheriff suddenly found a box on the floor and indicated to Rivers that he should come and look.

'Fuses!' Red smiled, patting the sheriff on the shoulder.

'There must be dynamite in here if there are fuses,' Romero said.

'The trouble is, where?' Red asked, scratching his whiskers.

It was like looking for a needle in a haystack.

★   ★   ★

Kid Palomino somehow managed to make his way across the empty room above the cantina as even more stray bullets smashed through the already broken window panes. The limping Kid

176

did not seem to care as slivers of glass showered over him before he reached the other side of the room and the small dresser which stood in the corner.

It was not the simple wooden piece of furniture that had drawn him like a moth to a flame, but the object that stood on its dusty surface.

Resting a hand on the dresser, Palomino picked up the ornate glass lamp and stared at the pint of oil inside the cut-crystal bowl.

He shook the lamp and watched as the yellow oil swirled around within its base.

It was not very much oil for the job he wanted it to do.

Would it be enough?

It had to be enough, he thought.

It took every ounce of the Kid's strength to reach the window again, but he managed it. Resting his sweat-soaked shirt on the cool adobe wall, he gasped as he carefully managed to remove the tall glass funnel. He tossed it on the floor, gritted his teeth and stared at the damp wick. He could smell the lamp oil fumes as he pulled out the box of matches and fumbled one of the wooden sticks from it.

There had not been a break of more than a few seconds in the gunfire since the rebels had stormed the barricade, he thought. As long as the rifles and pistols kept on being fired it meant that some of the good townspeople were still alive.

It was the screams that chilled him, though. Hideous screams which came up from the street as the battle continued below the balcony.

Palomino knew he had to act quickly. He had to buy some time for the inexperienced citizens of San Remo while there were still some of them left to save. They were being slaughtered by men who relished fighting and had no fear of dying.

Palomino ran his thumbnail across the tip of the match and watched as it exploded into flame in his cupped bloodstained hand. When the flame had steadied, he touched it to the moist wick of the lamp. Then he blew out the match.

The lamp-wick was burning well in the gentle breeze that drifted through the open window at his side.

The Kid clambered out of the window on to the balcony, staying low as he held on to the heavy glass lamp. He moved to the edge of the wooden parapet and cautiously looked down into the street at the upturned buckboards and water-barrels which made up the meagre defences. The barricade had been pushed over ten feet away from where it had originally been situated and was now directly beneath him.

As the Kid cast his eyes over the street, he felt physically sick. It was a lurid sight. Bodies seemed to be strewn everywhere on the blood-soaked ground.

Palomino whistled down at the men below him.

'Take cover up the street,' he shouted

at what was left of his valiant force. They did not seem to require telling twice and began to scatter in all directions.

Palomino turned the small brass wheel on the side of the lamp until the flame was over three inches high, then threw it with all his force straight down on to the tinder-dry wooden barricade. The glass bowl shattered into a dozen fragments when it hit the barricade, sending burning oil spilling over the closest of the upturned vehicles.

Fire seemed to wash over the bullet-riddled buckboard.

Flames suddenly engulfed it and spread quickly across the length of the improvised obstacles. Choking black smoke billowed into the air like a living, blinding curtain.

For the first time since Zeb Coltrane's Raiders had entered San Remo, they were actually backing their mounts away from the barricade. The flames swirled and spat furiously from the burning wood, filling the street with the putrid black smoke.

As Kid Palomino crawled through the window, a volley of lethal bullets sprayed all around him.

He fell to the floor of the room, and heard the sound of men entering the cantina directly below him. Their angry voices echoed up the stairs.

They were coming for him.

18

Bullets blasted from the guns of the three battle-weary rebels as they reached the top of the stairs and faced the strangely silent area. Fanning the hammers of their pistols, the men walked into the room directly above the cantina and suddenly realized that their quarry had somehow fled.

The first of the raiders hastily moved across the bare board floor, holding his smoking pair of Remingtons. He stopped next to one of the windows. Smoke was now being blown in through the shattered wooden frame from the still blazing inferno which stretched across the main street.

As his two companions reached his side they paused.

'I seen him coming in here through that damn window,' the first man insisted, waving one of his guns.

The second man coughed. 'Well he ain't here.'

'Are you plumb sure that you done seen a man coming in through that window?' the third man asked.

As the first man moved away from the choking smoke he spotted the spilled blood covering the boards.

'Is that blood or am I loco?'

The third man stooped and ran his fingers through the sticky mess. He rubbed it between his fingers.

'It's blood OK.'

The first man marched to the second window and poked his head out to look at the balcony. Bloody footprints led away from the window to the very edge of the balcony.

'I got me a trail, boys,' he said. He followed the tracks out on to the balcony. His cohorts followed him to the very end of the balcony and stared at the building next to it. Its roof was only a few feet lower than the balcony on which they were standing. Bloody boot marks below them showed that their prey had fled this way.

'He must have been wounded.'

'Unless that weren't his blood.'

'He must have gotten back to street level by now.'

The sweating man was right. Kid Palomino had managed to clamber down from the balcony on to the roof of the adjoining building unseen by anyone as the black smoke obscured him. Then he'd dropped into an alley.

'We'll find him later,' the first rebel said.

The three men turned and started back towards the window they had only just emerged from. Then they all noticed something away in the prairie beyond the heat-haze.

Dust was rising from beyond the tall cactus along the trail they had used only minutes earlier.

'What is it, Zeb?'

Coltrane spat out at the distant shimmering images. Images he knew only too well. Even through the heat-haze of the early morning sun, he could see the bluecoats he had grown to hate with every ounce of his being, riding toward San Remo.

Before the leader of the ruthless remnants of a once proud army could reply, the sound of a bugle came echoing from the prairie.

'Come on. We better gather what's left of the men together and ride,' Coltrane screamed as he followed his long leg in through the window and began running for the stairs.

As the three reached the street flames leapt at them from what was left of the barricade. The heat forced them back as the fire ignited the wooden upright and then the balcony above their heads.

'What we gonna do, Zeb?' one of the men yelled as he was forced back by the intense heat of the fire which was preventing them from reaching what was left of their men and also their trusty mounts.

Zeb Coltrane's mind raced.

For the first time in all the years he had ridden at the head of his band of

Confederate rebels, he found himself separated from them.

For the first time, Coltrane was frightened.

He could hear his men calling pitifully to him from beyond the black billowing smoke as it choked them. Yet he could no longer see even one of them. The flames spat viciously at the three grey coated raiders as they stood helplessly trapped on the wrong side of the blazing barricade.

'What we gonna do, Zeb?' one of the two men standing next to him asked.

Coltrane glanced silently at the rebel.

Then he heard his remaining riders galloping away in the direction of the approaching Union troop. The bugle seemed to get louder and louder; then the distant shooting started. For a few seconds there was nothing but the noise of gunfire in their ears.

It did not last long.

Zeb Coltrane's eyes darted in every direction as he raced across the wide street toward the sheriff's office with the last two of his men on his heels. It was not easy for tired legs to avoid the carnage spread out all about them. The bodies of men and horses were scattered everywhere.

The three entered the smoke-filled office and soon located what they were looking for. The wall-mounted rifle-rack and the bureau below it.

Coltrane grabbed the last two remaining Winchesters off the rack and tossed them to the two confused men at his side. Opening the small doors of the bureau, Coltrane pulled out the boxes of various calibre bullets and checked them.

As Zeb Coltrane and the last of his rebels cautiously moved back out into the smoke-filled street, they had all the ammunition they required.

Yet they were trapped.

'We've gotta find horses,' Coltrane said, moving through the smoke along the boardwalk at the head of his tiny force. One of the men pointed over Coltrane's shoulder down to the far end of the long street. Even with the smoke hindering their view, they could see horses tied up near the last of the adobe buildings.

'Look, Zeb. Horses.'

Coltrane loaded his guns and studied the buildings between them and the horses. There were still men with rifles lying in wait, he thought. Yet as he glanced over his shoulder at the still raging fire that blocked the entire width of the street, he began to smile.

'What you smiling for, Zeb?'

Zeb Coltrane cocked the hammers of his Remingtons again and spat the acrid taste of smoke at the ground. He knew that whoever had started that blaze had probably saved their lives because even the US Cavalry could not ride through fire.

'Keep alert, men. Kill anything that moves. We're gonna get us some horses and ride out of here.'

19

Kid Palomino favoured his leg as he staggered from the narrow alley up the side of the bank toward the main street. He had hurt his injured leg dropping from the roof of the single-storey building next to the cantina but knew he had to try and get back to the sheriff's office. He needed a carbine if he was going to keep the rebels far enough away from him so that they could not take advantage of his inability to move quickly. He also needed bullets for his prized pair of matched Colts.

Leaning on the brown wall on the corner of the main street he searched his gunbelt for bullets for his guns. He realized it was a vain venture when his fingers traced the empty leather loops of the belt.

Checking his left hand pistol he noted it held only three .45 cartridges whilst his right had five.

Eight bullets in two guns was running too close to the wind for Kid Palomino. He holstered both weapons and removed his Stetson before looking around the corner down the length of the street.

Then he saw them.

Zeb Coltrane and the last two of his men were cautiously making their way along the opposite boardwalk. The Kid then saw the smoke and flames leaping from the wooden frontage of the cantina. Even though the morning breeze was gentle, the fire was being fanned more than enough for it to spread.

What had he started? Kid Palomino wondered if setting light to the barricade had been such a good idea after all. His only consolation was the fact that the bodies of the building were made of sod. That at least should not catch fire, even if all the porches and roofs caught alight, he mused.

Palomino could see the condition of

what remained of San Remo's menfolk as they huddled together directly opposite the bank where he stood.

'Get to your families and get out of town,' Palomino shouted at the men as he waved his left arm frantically.

They did not wait for him to change his mind. He watched as they scurried down the lane and disappeared behind the back of the adobe building. At least there were still enough of them to take their wives and children to safety, he thought as he glanced at the three slow-moving rebels.

Black smoke billowed and twisted its way around the wide street as flames ignited the wooden boardwalk and porch overhangs behind the renegade soldiers.

Soon it was difficult to see the approaching men clearly as they continued their advance.

Kid Palomino wondered why they were coming in his direction and not trying to get around the fire and to their waiting men and horses.

Horses!

That was it, the Kid thought. They were coming for fresh horses. They must have spotted the horses he had ordered to be tied up at the far end of town, well away from where the fighting was to happen.

Then Palomino heard the cavalry bugle echoing out beyond the leaping flames. That was no rebel bugle call, he thought. Only the Union forces used that particular version of the melodic order to charge. Palomino was no soldier but knew that no son of Dixie was blowing that tune. Suddenly he felt a great weight being lifted from his staggering frame. The cavalry must have been trailing the Confederate riders and, by the sound of it, had defeated all those on the other side of the fiery barricade.

The Kid drew his right hand Colt and cocked its hammer, gritting his teeth against the intense pain which ripped through his body. Only three of them left, he muttered to himself under his breath as he straightened up. Three men against the eight bullets in his pair of pearl-handled guns.

There was a chance he just might not need that extra ammunition or a rifle. There was a chance he might live to see another sunset.

As he licked his dry lips, Kid Palomino readied himself to step out into the street and face the approaching killers. Taking a deep breath, he was about to move when he heard a noise behind him. For a second, the young deputy froze as he heard the two sets of feet moving closer.

Reluctantly the Kid turned his head and looked over his shoulder. Then he saw the two men standing with their rifles gripped firmly in their hands.

'Jones?' Palomino questioned the older man who had the barrel of his Winchester aimed directly at the tin star pinned to his vest.

'The name's Jim Welch, Palomino,' Welch growled, screwing up his eyes and staring hard at the tall man. 'Drop the six-shooter.'

Kid Palomino loosened his grip on the Colt and allowed it to fall into the sand at his feet.

'What's wrong, boys?'

Welch glanced at Ben Black at his side and smirked.

'See, Ben. This is the dude who killed Hoyt and the rest of our boys back in Juárez.'

'Him?' Black still did not believe that anyone who looked like Palomino could possibly be of any use with his guns. 'He don't look like he could outdraw Hoyt or anyone else for that matter, Jim. He can't be the guy.'

Jim Welch stepped closer.

'Did you kill my brother Hoyt and our gang?'

Kid Palomino felt sweat trickling down the side of his face.

'Maybe. There have been so many that it's hard to keep track of them all.'

Welch jabbed the rifle barrel hard

into Palomino's belly, forcing the deputy to bend double in pain. As the Kid saw the well-built man raising his Winchester to bring down on the back of his skull, he acted.

Faster than either man had ever seen a gun drawn, Palomino pulled his left-hand pistol from its holster and fired. Welch staggered backwards for three paces before collapsing at the feet of his partner. Black swung the barrel of his carbine around in Kid Palomino's direction and fired.

As the bullet skimmed across the fabric of the deputy's shirt, the Kid reluctantly squeezed his trigger again. Ben Black was thrown six feet backwards as the bullet snuffed out his pitiful existence.

Kid Palomino turned around quickly and moved back to the corner of the building again. As the smoke lifted from the main street he felt his heart starting to race. The three men were no longer walking down the boardwalk on the opposite site side of the wide main street. The shots had alerted them to his presence, he thought.

Where were they?

Where had they gone?

Finale

A merciless sun blazed down on the scene of total carnage. Kid Palomino knew he had to make a move if he was to have any chance of survival. Somewhere out in the smoke-filled street, three ruthless hardened killers knew exactly where he was. The three shots had alerted them not only to his presence, but also his exact position.

The Kid grabbed one of the rifles off the ground and limped as fast as he could down the alley. He had to try and get around the back of this large building, the last in the long line of buildings on this side of the street and make his way to the schoolhouse. That was where he suspected Red had hidden not only the townspeople's horses, but Derby and Nugget.

If that was where the three rebels were headed, the Kid knew that would be his best chance of stopping them.

As he rounded the corner of the building and tried to increase his speed through the soft sand, Palomino heard the sound of men behind him once again.

His blood ran cold.

Had they gotten the drop on him before he had a chance of doing the same to them? Kid Palomino gripped the bloody rifle in his hands and let his index finger slide over its trigger.

Turning with the rifle in his hands, the Kid had almost fired when he recognized Red and Romero running towards him, carrying a box between them. As he lowered the rifle barrel, Palomino felt every nerve in his body twitching.

'You OK, Palomino?' Red asked as he and the sheriff reached the sweating younger man.

'I almost shot you both,' the Kid gasped.

'We got it,' Ned Romero said eagerly,

pushing the box beneath Kid Palomino's nose.

Kid Palomino stared at the half-dozen sticks of dynamite and equal number of fuses. Then he looked at the faces of his two fellow lawmen.

'I thought you were going to use this on them rebels?'

'Weren't no need. The cavalry showed up and they're still rounding up what's left of the varmints.' Red smiled broadly. 'Guess it's all over.'

Palomino allowed the man with the red beard to support him.

'Nope, it ain't over. There are still three of them out there somewhere, boys.'

The sheriff's face went pale.

'Good job we brought this stuff with us.'

Kid Palomino nodded.

'We have to get to where you left the horses, Red.'

'I left them all tied up in the field behind the school building, Kid,' Red said. The three men headed towards the end of the street.

Suddenly as the trio of law-officers reached the corner directly across from the whitewashed school, they were stopped in their tracks.

Bullets flew at them with venomous ferocity as they saw the three riders appearing from behind the school-house. Zeb Coltrane was astride Red Rivers' brown quarter horse Derby, waving his deadly sabre above his head. One of his men was riding the tall palomino stallion Nugget and the other rebel rode a black gelding.

Coltrane's men fired their guns at the sheriff and his two deputies as they thundered past them.

'They got our horses, Kid,' Red said. They ducked back behind the solid wall of the building whilst the riders urged their mounts out in the direction of the vast prairie.

Kid Palomino leaned against the wall and placed his fingers in his mouth. The whistle was loud and clear.

Red Rivers and Romero gasped in

amazement as they saw Nugget stop galloping and then rear up into the air. The rebel fell from the saddle, still shooting his pistol until he hit the ground.

'How do you get that horse of yours to do things like that?' Red asked as they made their way towards the stunned rebel.

Kid Palomino raised his rifle and aimed carefully. He fired once and took the rider off the back of the black gelding. As he cranked the mechanism of the Winchester he saw Coltrane disappearing over a sandy rim into the jungle of Joshua trees.

'That critter got my horse, Palomino,' Red said throwing his hat on to the ground angrily.

Without saying a word, Kid Palomino limped to Nugget's side and gathered up the loose reins. Grabbing a handful of the creamy mane in his right hand, he stepped into his stirrup and hauled himself on top of the tall stallion.

'I'll get that old nag of yours, Red,' Palomino said. He tapped his spurs into the side of his mount and thundered after the rebel leader.

Urging the stallion after the tracks left by his partner's quarter horse, the Kid was about to let the huge stallion have his head when he saw something glinting through the prairie vegetation ahead of him.

He reined Nugget to a halt and waited as he saw something coming slowly towards him. Nervously, he drew the gun from his right holster and rested it on the silver-topped saddle horn as he waited for the rider to reach the clearing.

Kid Palomino saw the gleaming bloodstained sabre first and felt his finger resting on the trigger of his Colt. Then, as his eyes focused, the Kid recognized the proud features of Blue Snow riding his painted pony whilst leading Red's horse behind him. The Comanche warrior dropped the sabre. Both men watched as its blade stuck in the ground between their two mounts.

'The man who was riding Red's horse?' Palomino questioned.

'Him leader of men who killed my brothers. Him now dead.' Blue Snow handed Derby's reins over to Kid Palomino before turning his painted pony and galloping off into the dense undergrowth.

Looking down at the sabre for a few seconds, Kid Palomino knew that this time it was really over. He pulled hard on Nugget's reins and turned the magnificent stallion around. He headed back towards San Remo with the brown quarter horse following close behind.

'Did ya get the varmint, Palomino?' Red called out, rushing towards his beloved horse. 'Is he dead?'

'He's dead all right but it wasn't me who got him,' the Kid replied as he reached the two lawmen.

'Then who killed him?' Ned Romero asked, looking up into the eyes of the young deputy.

'The best man me and Red have ever

met, Ned,' Kid Palomino answered. A smile began to trace across his face.

'Blue Snow?' Red asked.

Kid Palomino looked across at Major Joseph Saunders leading what remained of his cavalry troop toward them.

'Yep.' He said.

Other titles in the
Linford Western Library:

THE CHISELLER

Tex Larrigan

Soon the paddle steamer would be on its long journey down the Missouri River to St Louis. Now, all Saul Rhymer had to do was to play the last master stroke of the evening. He looked at the mounting pile of gold and dollar bills and again at the cards in his hand. Then, looking around the table, he produced the deed to the goldmine in Montana. 'Let's play poker!' But little did he know how that journey back to St Louis would change his life so drastically.